SIX TALES FROM PURGATORY

SIX TALES FROM PURGATORY

PAUL S. FOWLER

ISBN: 978-0-578-46580-7

For Kimberly

Contents

THE BROOKIE

The place looked as if it had been untouched. Not untouched for a time, but truly untouched—pristine. The loggers' saws and axes had not been here. The white oaks growing on the upper edge of the limestone canyon were hoary and ancient and of massive girth. The place was more of a box canyon, about 150 yards long. It began at an opening in the mountain, a small, low cave from which the spring issued forth. Rhododendron grew on the steep sloped walls of the canyon almost to the edge of the stream, which itself was no more than twenty feet wide and as narrow as ten. The walls of the canyon were highest at the mouth of the cave, perhaps fifty feet, and dropped to around twenty feet high at the canyon's exit. The stream was more or less level along its length until it once again disappeared into the mountain, its exit a jumble of limestone boulders around which the water had to flow in order to continue underground to the river far below. The place was well covered by the canopy of hardwoods, and sunlight entered it only in shafts, giving it a sylvan and mysterious atmosphere. The fisherman had made his way up from the Dry Fork River, beginning his journey early in the morning. The climb had been hard going. From the edge of the river, access to this area of the spring was guarded by dense briar thickets, a combination of greenbriers, multiflora roses, and blackberries. The fisherman had been obliged to cut his way into the mess with nippers and a machete, often resorting to crawling through the narrow passages. The first hundred yards or so were fairly level and ended at the base of the mountain, which rose steeply from the river valley. The first leg of the ascent passed through relatively open mixed hardwoods and was easy going despite the grade. After that, the laurel began, sparse at first but becoming a nearly impenetrable mass. The grade as well as the tangle of laurel made further ascent painfully slow and laborious. The fisherman would cut, nip, crawl, and take a breather. He knew he was close when he found a very old four-strand barbed-wire fence. Behind the fence was a stacked stone wall overgrown with laurel. From what he had learned looking at the tax map at the county courthouse, this had to be the property he was looking for.

The fisherman had always speculated about the origins of the limestone springs that fed the Dry Fork. His curiosity had led him to do some research, and he had pored over topographical maps and satellite imagery of the area above the river. He'd found a curious anomaly in the topography of the mountain. It appeared there was a small, deep canyon about halfway up. A feature like this could mean only one thing in his mind—flowing water. A trip to the assessor's office had revealed the canyon was located on a thirty-five-and-a-half-acre parcel owned by a group called "The Preservation Society." Intrigued, the fisherman had researched further and found that the earliest recorded deed holder for the property was a man named Oliver Purcell. In 1803, Purcell had originally been granted around five hundred acres, of which the canyon area had been a part. Purcell was an interesting character, having been a blockade runner during the revolution and then a successful land speculator in the early years of the republic. Purcell had managed to amass a fortune through land and real estate dealings. He'd built an estate in northern Virginia, and the five-hundred-acre parcel had passed to his son and then to his grandson. All but the thirty-five-acre parcel had been sold during the timber rush in the new state of West Virginia following the Civil War. Oliver Purcell's grandson Peter, who was well educated and was said to have had a keen interest in archeological mysteries, had left the land to the Preservation Society under the condition that the land "be secured from the public" and that "the Indian and natural wonders be preserved for the benefit of all." The transfer of the land to the Preservation Society had taken place in 1927, and there was little mention of it after that time, save that it had been fenced by hired locals in 1928. Fencing was likely unnecessary as the terrain and laurel were so formidable, locals never ventured there. There were far easier places to hunt or cut timber.

There were far easier places to fish as well. The fisherman had not been deterred by the extreme effort it was taking to reach this spot, even while being assailed by greenbriers or crawling on his belly beneath laurel up the steep mountainside. He had fished all of the easier places. He had fished almost every river in the area, and there were many. He reveled in casting flies to the wild brookies and browns and the beauty and solitude of the places they called home. As he'd grown older, he'd begun to place more of a premium on the purity of the experience, getting to the point where he would leave a stretch of water at the sight of another fisherman. It mattered most to him that the time he spent on the water was his own and that the fish he caught were wild. He shuddered when he thought of places where, at the appointed time, people would stand elbow to elbow to catch steelhead, salmon, or trout. In the spring, he would look with disdain on the caravans on the road following the trout-stocking truck waiting for its pale, pellet-fed cargo to be disgorged into the river. Fellowship had never been his bag, save for the times he'd fished with his wife or son. Some of his fondest memories were of evenings spent on the water with his wife. The two of them would often fish well into dusk, to the point that they would set their hooks to the sound of a rise. His wife fished very seldom now, and he suspected she fished more to be with him than because she liked to fish. Barring fishing with her or his son, he preferred to fish alone. He had read of early expeditions into the Blackwater where men had caught ridiculous numbers of native brook trout and wished he could have fished such waters. Time and the onslaught of mining and logging had erased those possibilities, unless this place, sheltered from human progress for so long, held what he hoped for. If there was running water up there, a length of stream able to hold brook trout, it would be a once-in-a-lifetime chance to step back to an earlier age.

The fence was hardly an obstacle. The wire was so rusted and frail, it gave way with a little effort. The stone wall was reminiscent of those he had seen in parts of New England, but higher and wider. He found a section damaged by a fallen tree and was able to cross it using the tree trunk as a ramp. Once on the other side, he gauged the width of the wall at about five feet, and taking into account the depth of the forest litter, he estimated its original height at around eight or ten feet. The fisherman wondered who had built the wall. The land was never really settled, and the first deed was sold back in 1803, so he surmised native people must have built it. Being relatively familiar with the tribes that hunted the area, mostly Shawnee and Iroquois, he was reasonably sure it was not their handiwork. He had never heard of those tribes building anything in stone. He knew there were large earthworks, or mounds as they were called in other parts of West Virginia—perhaps it was these people who had built the wall. For a few moments, he took in the aura of the area inside. The place was rocky with some immense limestone boulders, some as big as cars, jutting out of the earth. Huge oaks and hickories towered overhead, and he was sure they were old growth. The laurels seemed to have thinned on this side of the wall, as though they, too, were compelled to stay out. The ground was more level here, and he was glad. It seemed the worst was behind him.

He moved ahead, deciding to push farther away from the wall and continue ascending. He quickly picked up a deer trail that wound between the boulders and the trees and decided to follow it. At this point, there was little understory, and he could see ahead fairly well. As he was passing between two particularly huge boulders, he noticed that the flat face of the boulder to his left had been carved. Even with the lichen, it was possible to make out a large spiral-shaped carving in the center, like a sun perhaps, surrounded by indecipherable petroglyphs. As he studied the stone, he ran his hand over the carved surface. Water and lichen had done their work, but the carvings were deep and had therefore survived. In this quiet moment, he heard it, unmistakable—the sound of running water. The spell of the carvings broken, he hurried forward on the path, and as he did, the sound of running water grew stronger. The slope of the mountain seemed to be rising to his right. He came to another huge boulder, carved much the same as the one he had just seen. The water was very close, but he still could not see it. The air had become cooler, another sign he was near a flowing spring. The game path led around the right side of the boulder, and he was once again faced with a section of stone wall. This section was short, running about twenty feet from the edge of the boulder to the slope of the mountain. The wall was down in the center. It looked as if it might have been pulled down long ago as the leaf litter had all but obscured the pile of stones that formed a ramp at its base. With a few steps, he was through the gap.

The stream. He had been right. At this point, the water was about fifteen feet wide and maybe a couple of feet deep at most. To his left, he saw the end of the stream where the water moved around the rock and disappeared underground, apparently right under the huge, carved boulder at the entrance. As he studied the stream's termination point, his eyes caught something vaguely familiar to him. Half buried in the sediment of the bank near him was the unmistakable profile of a fly reel. For a moment, he felt deflated. Someone else had been fishing here. Yet he had found no other sign to indicate human travel. He'd been forced to literally cut his way up from the river. He dropped his pack and stepped to the edge of the stream, kneeling to reach the reel. With a little effort, he freed the relic from the gravel. The reel was still attached to the broken butt-section of a rod. Bamboo. Cane. The rod was very old. The reel was small, made of steel, and the line remaining on it appeared to be the old, braided silk stuff. No one had used fly tackle like this for a long time—at least fifty years. He breathed a sigh of relief. Someone else had been here, but not for a very long time. He leaned the artifact against a big rock by the stream's edge, intending to take it back home with him as a souvenir. The fisherman checked the time on his wristwatch. It was almost nine o'clock. It had taken him about three hours to get here. He stepped back to his pack and pulled out a few items. First his fly rod—a three-piece, six-and-a-half-foot, three weight that he used for fishing out-of-the-way brook trout streams—and then a reel and a fly box filled with a broad assortment of flies, and finally a bottle of water and some granola bars. He had learned long ago that it is always wise to take some time and study the water before you begin casting flies. He sat down with his back against a rock, took a drink of water, opened a granola bar, and took a bite. In the excitement of finding this place, he hadn't realized how hungry he was.

He was only halfway through the granola bar when he saw the first rise. The surface of the water along the length of stream was not calm, but smooth enough that he could spot a rise easily. Within a few minutes, he saw many other fish rising up and down the length of water. There were some rises that indicated sizable fish too. He finished the granola bar, drained the bottle of water, placed the trash in his pack, and began rigging up. With efficiency that was second nature, he assembled the rod, attached the reel, and fed the fly line through the eyes, being careful not to miss any. That done, he pulled a small envelope from his pack containing a new seven-and-a-half-foot 5X tapered leader, formed a loop in the butt end, and attached it to his fly line. As he straightened the leader by pulling it between his fingers, he kept an eye on the action. He noticed small, dark mayflies emerging from the water sporadically. Not a big hatch, but one of those that happens from time to time through the daylight hours from May through July. His leader straightened to his satisfaction, he opened his fly box, selected a #16 Adams Parachute, and tied it on. The fish were still rising here and there, so the fisherman found a lie behind a stone in the stream, and after casting upstream and slightly to the left of the spot, he set his fly down on the water gently. The fly drifted about a foot when it was taken hard. The fisherman set the hook. From the feel of it, this was a good fish. Upon bringing the fish to heel, he was not disappointed. The brookie was stout twelve incher, very dark. Almost every cast produced similar results. The fish were universally darker than the brookies he had seen elsewhere, and he speculated whether they had evolved that way because of the isolation. He thought for a moment that this could be a totally new subspecies. Such academic thoughts were soon lost to the nonstop action. He lost count of the fish he had caught and released after fifteen or so, never changing out the Adams he had tied on. Most of the fish were in the ten- to twelve-inch range with several being about fifteen to sixteen inches. These trout had never seen an artificial fly, so they attacked his offerings with utter recklessness.

The fisherman worked his way slowly up the creek. The banks on either side were relatively clear, so apart from crossing the stream a few times to get into a better position to cast, he didn't have to do any wading, for which he was grateful as even brook trout that have never seen a fisherman are notoriously spooky, and the water was exceptionally cold. The stream flowed in a slight bend, so it was not until early afternoon that the fisherman could see the source of the stream—that low cave coming out of the very heart of the mountain. He fished toward it slowly, methodically catching yet more of the dark brookies and letting them go. He seldom used a net, preferring to handle the fish with his wet hands to prevent damage to their protective layer of slime, the exception being fish too large to land easily by hand. As he neared the last thirty feet of the stream, the fishing died down. Although the area around the mouth of the cave looked promising—a pool about four or five feet deep and about twenty feet wide—there were no rising fish. The fisherman paused to watch the pool. The bottom being very dark, it would be hard to spot a brookie unless it was moving near the surface. The walls of the canyon grew steep in this last stretch, so the only casting position would be from the front of the pool. As it was close, it would present no problem. The sun was at the point where the canyon would be losing direct sunlight soon, even though it would not be dark till around eight or so. Near the mouth of the cave, he saw something swim through a shaft of light in the water. He kept watching, and to his amazement, he saw the form of a huge brookie come close to the surface of the water. In his estimation (and he had seen a lot of trout), the fish was at least twenty inches long. He could clearly see the white and black of its fins and that its belly was a deep red. It hovered near the surface for a minute and then slowly settled into a hold near the bottom of the creek. The water being crystal clear, it was an easy thing to see the fish, but the fisherman knew that had he not watched the brookie settle into this lie, it would be hard to spot it because of the camouflage-like vermiculations on the trout's back.

He stood for a few minutes watching the big fish holding steady near the rock. He figured the water there was about three feet deep and that the current was fairly even on the surface. The fisherman considered tying on a different fly, maybe something bigger that might be more enticing to such a brute, but with the daylight starting to wane, he decided against it. The cast would be short, about twenty feet, but he would have to take into account a large oak log lying halfway in the water, blocking the left side of the pool. After a few more moments of consideration, he decided to take a chance and wade out a little farther toward the center of the stream. Moving almost painfully slowly, the fisherman moved to the center of the stream, the cold water flowing around his bare legs, watching to ensure the ripples from his movement were kept to a minimum. Once he was satisfied with his position, he looked at the hold to try and spot the fish. After a few moments, he was able to make out the form of the brookie. It hadn't moved and was still lying near the bottom, finning lazily. The fisherman made a few false casts until he was satisfied he had the distance he needed; he then cast the fly about ten feet above and to the left of the trout. The fly landed softly on the surface, hardly making a ripple. Before the fisherman had a chance to react, the big trout darted to the surface and hit the fly. The fisherman raised the rod tip to set the hook, later than he should have, but the power of the fish's strike made the action unnecessary. The hook was set on the strike, and the fish immediately dove to the bottom of the pool and made a run toward the darkness of the cave mouth. The reel's drag was singing, and the fisherman knew he couldn't let the big trout get too far down into the cave. He palmed the rim of the spool, slowing and then stopping the fish. The rod bent under the pressure, and the fisherman worried that the tippet would give way to the trout's strength. The fish then darted back out toward the fisherman. He reeled furiously, trying to get as much line back onto the reel as possible. As he reeled, he began to move closer to the center of the pool, closing the distance between him and the fish. The fisherman kept the pressure on, just enough to slow the trout down without breaking off. He wondered how he would be able to tire the fish out enough in this small space. There was not much room, and there were numerous hazards that the trout might get into and tangle up his leader. He decided to try and move the fish to the right side of the pool as he thought it clearer and less likely to give the fish something to tangle up on. The brookie was holding its ground now, not bulldogging or making another wild run. The fisherman waded to his right, keeping pressure on the fish. His rod was held to the right as well, almost perpendicular to the water and bent nearly double. He could feel the fish moving with him like a dead weight being drawn slowly through the water. He turned to face the fish, its form visible but distorted. He was surprised the trout had given up the fight so quickly, but in the moment, he concentrated more on landing it. The fisherman reeled in until only a foot of his floating line remained outside of the guide on the rod's tip; then, he raised the rod high above him, extending his right arm fully, reaching backward as though he were stretching. While he did this, he reached back with his left hand and grabbed his net. The fish was very close now, within ten feet or so, and the man noticed something odd about it—it was stiff, somehow lifeless-looking. It was at that moment he felt something brush against his left leg. Having been a fly fisherman his whole life, the man had no innate aversion to the water or the creatures that lived in it, but this was different. Something solid was moving against his leg. He took his eyes off the fish for a moment and glanced down quickly. A black tentacle was sliding around his leg. A wave of revulsion set in, and he felt the blood drain from his face. The fish was still on the line; the fisherman's right arm was raised above him, holding the rod. With a start, he dropped his rod and attempted to run, to get out of the water. The tentacle clamped around his leg, and he felt a searing pain shoot up his calf. Groping forward, the fisherman lunged toward the edge of the pool in a blind panic. As he did, he felt another tentacle close around his right leg, followed by the same pain. He was screaming, his cries filling the small canyon. The tentacles yanked his legs out from under him, and he found himself facedown in the water—in the water with this *thing*. He struggled, trying to hold on to something, anything, but to no avail. He felt himself being pulled farther into the pool, into the deeper water, into the darkness of the cave. The pain in his legs was gone, but he now felt himself going limp, helpless. Try as he might, the man could not will his body to move. Another tentacle wrapped around his neck, and with a last burst of strength, he screamed, screamed into the water as his lungs filled. The appendage that he'd thought was a brook trout moved past his eyes. As he was pulled into the cave, he saw that the stream bed just outside the cave mouth was littered with bones. Trapped within his limp body, trapped with only his horror, the fisherman's eyes focused on a beam of light, the last he would ever see, penetrating the dappled water, and with that, he lapsed into blackness.

LILITH'S DAUGHTER

With several files and a clipboard in one hand and her briefcase in the other, Sheila struggled to push open the heavy glass-and-aluminum door. Two men stood just outside, watching Sheila as they smoked. When she had the door halfway open, Sheila struggled to squeeze through. As she did, the clipboard fell from her grasp and clattered onto the sidewalk. Sheila briefly looked at the two men, one of whom returned her glance and went back to chatting with his companion. Sheila held the door open with her back as she squatted down, trying to reach the wayward clipboard lying on the damp concrete. The brown polyester of her slacks stretched tightly over her legs and buttocks as her fingers inched toward it. One of the men nudged the other with his elbow and gestured toward Sheila. The two watched with obvious amusement, hoping for further catastrophe. Sheila was finally able to grasp the clipboard, and with a last burst of effort, she righted herself and pushed around the door. Red-faced from the exertion, Sheila trundled past the two smokers toward the parking lot. As she reached the curb, she heard one of the men exclaim, "Christ, what a wide load!" and laughter followed.

Sheila considered saying something to them in return, something deriding their manhood or manners, but she let it go. Sheila always let these things go. Experience told her it was better to pretend not to hear the taunts and insults. Short and pudgy, with thin hair and small eyes, Sheila would never be considered a great beauty. Sheila could more appropriately be described as unfortunate. Her unfortunate state extended beyond her appearance; she was shy and withdrawn to the point of being antisocial.

Sheila continued walking to the far end of the parking lot, the two men's snickering still in her ears. The sky had begun to spit a wet snow by the time she'd reached her car, a 1978 Ford LTD. Sheila placed her briefcase on the hood, fished her keys from the pocket of her slacks, and unlocked the door. The car, though aged, was in very good shape. Sheila's mother had put few miles on it, and Sheila only drove the car to work and back. It had been left to her along with her mother's house (the only home she had ever known) and the balance of her life insurance after funeral expenses and paying off a couple of small debts. Her mother had died unexpectedly a little over three years ago. The loss had been a crushing blow to Sheila. Her mother had been her best and only friend. Sheila was reminded of her mother each time she climbed into the old LTD. Countless drives to school where she had been bullied mercilessly by the other kids, weekend drives to the lake, Christmas shopping. She could picture her mother behind the wheel, singing along with the radio, the car seat padded by cushions so she could see over the dashboard. Sheila had never known her father, and she and her mother had only spoken of the man once.

Sheila turned the key, and the old car's engine roared to life. She adjusted the heat to defrost and sat there waiting for the car's engine to warm up—very important, according to her mother, another bit of advice she had taken in and kept. Her mother had been her sole advisor, a true confidant. The morning of her mother's passing, Sheila awoke to an alien world. As far back as she could remember, Sheila's mother had roused her each morning. At the time of her mother's death, she'd been thirty-five and had held a job since graduating from college. She had even lived at home during her attendance because of the proximity of her mother's house to campus. But that morning, Sheila woke up alone.

After getting herself out of bed, Sheila opened her bedroom door, walked into the hall, and listened. The house was dark, and neither the smell of coffee nor breakfast wafted up the stairs as it normally did. The house was silent as well. Sheila heard none of the familiar sounds coming from the kitchen downstairs. Her mother loved *Good Morning America* and watched it each morning on a thirteen-inch TV Sheila had bought her for Christmas one year. Sheila heard nothing, not *Good Morning America*, not the sound of cooking or her mother humming. Sheila turned away from the stairs and looked down the hall. Her mother's bedroom door loomed at the end of it. She studied the door in the early morning gloom. The old glass doorknob stood out sharply against the dark oak. Sheila looked for light under the door and saw none. She stood there for a long time, frozen in place, but finally began to walk down the hall toward the door, the sound of her house slippers against the hardwood floor deafening in the silence. When Sheila reached the door, she paused again and listened for several minutes. After hearing nothing, she rapped weakly on the door. "Mother?" Sheila called out softly.

Hearing no response, Sheila called out a bit louder. "Mother, are you up?"

After waiting a few moments, Sheila found her hand on the cold glass doorknob, and the door opened as if on its own power. She could not remember crossing the dimly lit room. She could only remember standing next to her mother's bed, looking down at her small form under the covers, and the yellow pall of her face. Her mother's skin had a rubbery, synthetic look, and her mouth was agape.

"Oh, no, Mother! Oh, no!" Sheila uttered, and for a long time, she simply stood there, rocking back and forth, tears streaming down her face.

Sheila had no friends, and her sole contact with others was through her work. Sheila had been working for the Department of Health and Human Services since she'd graduated from college. Her mother had approved. The job was stable with a decent chance for advancement since there was a high turnover of employees. Sheila had stuck with it, despite her social awkwardness, and had discovered that though she might be a pariah in the everyday world, she could wield real power in her position. After the first few nerve-racking home assessments, she'd realized that most people could be cowed by the threat of losing their children and being charged with child abuse or endangerment. For the really hard cases, she could always call on law enforcement to accompany her. Even with the realization of her newfound power, Sheila always strove to be professional in carrying out her duties. She became known as a fair but stern advocate for families and children. As her stock in the agency had grown, she'd been called upon to deal with the most difficult cases— those that other, less experienced or stolid case workers hadn't wanted to deal with. Given the high turnover of employees, Sheila's already large case load was often augmented by the work of those employees who unexpectedly quit. The present business at hand was one of these cases. Sheila had inherited it from a young woman who had worked briefly for DHHS but had left for a job with a wilderness therapy program out in Utah.

Sheila put the car in drive and pulled out of the parking lot. The weather report on the radio estimated several inches of snow by morning. It was 2:30 in the afternoon. Sheila guessed she would have time enough to complete her business before it got really bad. Besides, she had gotten studded tires put on a few days ago. The route to her destination took her down the main drag through town, and Sheila decided she should have a bite to eat before she headed out of the city limits. She saw the glowing Sonny Burger marquee and wheeled the LTD into the drive-through. Pulling up to the dingy-looking menu sign, Sheila rolled her window down. "Welcome to Sonny Burger!" a voice said over the tinny-sounding speaker. "Can I take your order?"

"I'll have two cheeseburgers, small fries, and a medium Coke," Sheila answered.

"I have two cheeseburgers, small fries, and a medium Coke. Can I interest you in a Sonny Shake, ma'am?"

"No, thank you."

"Okay, ma'am. Your total is five-thirty-three. Please pull up to the next window."

After paying for and receiving her order, Sheila pulled the car around to the lot and put it in park, leaving the engine idling and the heater on low. Sheila thought the drive-through was the greatest culinary invention ever. You could order whatever you wanted and eat it without worrying about being ogled. For a decidedly antisocial person like Sheila, it was perfect. Her ritual began as she placed the two burgers on the dash near the defroster vents to keep them warm. She then took a long pull from her Coke and began to eat her fries. To Sheila, there was nothing as delicious as hot, salty french fries and nothing as unpleasant as cold ones. With her fries in one hand, she popped open her briefcase, which lay on the passenger seat, and pulled out a file marked "Duvall." The case began when a Central Power employee, a meter reader, had contacted DHHS. According to the meter reader, he'd been at the side of a residence when he noticed "a kid, a little girl, staring at him out of one of the basement windows." He went on to describe the child as "maybe six or seven with long black hair and big dark eyes." The man was sure the child had been home alone. He had knocked on the front door and received no response, and there was no car in the drive. Unattended child aside, the man also reported, "The kid didn't say anything. She just stared at me. It kind of gave me the creeps."

While DHHS had no problem with "creepy kids," they did have a problem with parents leaving six- or seven-year-olds home alone, possibly locked in the basement, for unknown lengths of time. After checking the address through various sources, Sheila determined the home belonged to a woman named Summer Duvall, the widow of Danforth Duvall and mother of Lily Duvall. The case would have been run-of-the-mill, routine, had

Sheila not remembered a strange story that had run in the town paper, the *Sentinel*, about six years ago. After a trip to the local library to scan the newspaper microfilm, she'd found what she had been looking for.

After eating her meal, Sheila put the file back into her briefcase, tidied up the car, and pulled out onto the highway. As she drove north out of town, she considered the wisdom of what she was doing. No one knew where she was heading, which was against policy, and moreover, she had taken great pains to keep her research of the case from everyone at work. But Sheila enjoyed those true-crime shows and fancied herself a bit of detective, and the idea of a bit of mystery in her life really appealed to her.

The incident in question was the death of one Danforth Duvall, husband of Summer, father of Lily. The incident had been barely reported—no more than a few paragraphs in the middle of the local paper. But the headline had been enough to grab Sheila's attention: "Local Man Dies at Daughter's Birth." Nebulous, to be sure. The cause of death was reported as "sudden and apparently unexplained." There had been no follow-up to the story, though Sheila had looked for one. The article had stated Mr. Duvall had died within minutes of the birth of his daughter. When Sheila had inherited the Duvall file from her coworker, it hadn't taken her long to determine that these were *the* Duvalls. For Sheila the investigator, the first step had been to check the records for any other complaints against Summer Duvall. The motive for this was simple: Sheila would know if there had been a history of abuse or neglect, and this would set the pace for her activities. But Sheila had found nothing. This woman didn't even have a speeding ticket or a noise complaint. Moreover, the home seemed stable.

Sheila's gut told her the little girl was in no real danger, and she could proceed at a slower pace and without reporting her findings to her supervisors. Not that any of her findings so far would interest the DHHS. Sheila was looking for something more than a run-of-the-mill abuse or neglect case. She knew, or perhaps felt, that there was something deeper and darker in question here. Maybe it was just her longing for some kind of break from the monotony her life had become. If that was it, then why not? Why not have some excitement, some mystery, in her life? It was totally out of character for her, so the need or compulsion she felt was alien. While she could justify it on a conscious level, there was more to it than that.

The snow was coming down hard now, and as she drove through town, she could see the grocery store parking lot was full of folks rushing to get what they needed before the storm made the roads treacherous. She passed a couple of plow trucks as well, their yellow lights flashing warnings through the falling snow. The snow was starting to blanket the road in places, but Sheila never thought about turning back. As she drove, her thoughts again turned to her mother. She found herself thinking of her mother more often lately. Sheila remembered the one and only time she and her mother had fought. Sheila was in her second year of college and had found her spirituality. Her mother had never professed any thoughts or convictions about religion or matters of the spirit, so it had been one of those nonissues, like who Sheila's father was and what had happened between him and her mother. It had simply never come up. Sheila had been spending a lot of time thinking about spirituality and religion. Looking back, it was pretty clear to her that it was an issue of wanting to belong, of feeling alone and ostracized. She spoke to the priest at the local Catholic church and was soon taking classes to become Catholic. Sheila's mother said little at first, and in Sheila's excitement, she didn't notice her mother's silence when she spoke about her foray into religion. Things came to a head one day when Sheila's mother sat her down and gave her the third degree about her involvement with the church. Sheila was a bit bewildered and then angry at her mother's attitude. Wasn't she doing something positive?

"I'm just very worried about you, hon," her mother said.

"What on earth would you have to worry about, Mother?"

"Well, sometimes people aren't what they seem. You've turned out fine without the church so far. I just worry that you could be taken in."

Sheila thought about it for a moment and then answered. "Mom, I'm smart enough to make this decision. I'm not a child, you know."

"I know you're not a child, but you don't know how the world is. I've kept you safe all these years, haven't I?"

Sheila snapped at this. "That's what it is! You just want to keep me here with you! No wonder I don't have any friends! Well, I'm not letting you do it this time, Mother. You're just being selfish."

Sheila's mother slapped her. "The priest that fathered you got what he wanted from me and then just moved on to another parish. Probably on to another young, ignorant girl! I've always loved you. I've never let you down. I would give my life for you. I have given my life to you. Do you have any idea how alone I was?

How people turned their backs on me? How the precious church all but cast me out?"

With that, Sheila's mother turned and walked up the stairs. Sheila stood in place for a long time, stunned. The subject never came up again. Life returned to normal, routine. The knowledge of who her father had been and the circumstances of her conception were filed away in her mind, more evidence that she was less than others, that she didn't belong.

As Sheila reached the edge of town, traffic began to relax. It seemed most folks had chosen to get home and stay there. She felt a little crazy, literally riding into a storm. Her doubts were being pushed aside by the inexplicable need to go on, to finish what she had started. The point of no return had been about a week earlier. Following the trail of evidence, Sheila had discovered there was one person who had actually been present at the hospital when the Duvall incident had taken place. Sheila had very solid connections with the local police, and it was an easy thing to get her hands on a copy of the police report. The list of those present at West Memorial Hospital was short, and of those on the list, only one still lived in the area. Deborah Hill, who was now head nurse at West, had been on duty the night of Mr. Duvall's death. Nurse Hill, as she was known, was a force to be reckoned with, and at the hospital, the other nurses feared her, and the doctors respected her. She had been there for nearly twenty years and would be privy to any and all goings-on at the hospital, personal and professional.

It was with some trepidation that Sheila contacted Nurse Hill to see if she would be willing to speak about the events of that night. After all, according to all accounts, Nurse Hill was everything Sheila was not—confident, attractive (though not romantically involved with anyone people could remember), and powerful. To Sheila's surprise, Nurse Hill agreed to meet with her. Even over the phone, it was clear Nurse Hill was a woman in charge. She set the time of the meeting at midnight, saying that she started her shift at eleven and that "it took the first hour to get everyone on track." Midnight—the perfect time for clandestine meetings, Sheila thought. Sheila arrived at ten till midnight and nervously waited at the nurse's station to meet Nurse Hill. She felt like she was heading for an interrogation, though she was the one who would be asking the questions. She had dressed as professionally as she had the means to, unconsciously wanting to impress this woman she had never met. As she waited, Sheila was struck by the atmosphere of the place. At this hour, it was quiet except for the occasional stirring of the nurses and the periodic moan of a patient. The hospital was old, and the hum and slight flicker of the fluorescent lights overhead added to the somber mood of the place. At about a minute before midnight, Nurse Hill arrived at the nurse's station. She was everything Sheila had expected and more, tall and blond with a perfect jawline and ice-blue eyes. Sheila thought she had the eyes of a wolf.

"Sheila Ward?" Nurse Hill said, extending a hand to Sheila.

"Yes, and you must be Ms. Hill," Sheila replied, taking the hand offered.

After a brief handshake, Nurse Hill turned crisply and began walking down a corridor to the north of the nurse's station. "This way, please, Ms. Ward," Nurse Hill said over her shoulder as she walked. The corridor seemed to be more dimly lit than the main hallway. As Sheila followed Nurse Hill, she caught glimpses of patients through the open doorways. Sheila could hear feeble moaning coming from a room just ahead to her right. As she passed the doorway, she paused and glanced in. Lying in the bed closest to the door, Sheila could see what appeared to be an elderly woman. The woman was moaning and feebly moving her head from side to side; then, unexpectedly, the woman turned her head quickly and looked at Sheila. In that moment, Sheila saw the face of her mother smiling at her. She gasped and stepped back.

"Are you coming, Ms. Ward?" Nurse Hill called to her. Sheila snapped out of it and looked at Nurse Hill, who had stopped, looking back at her. Sheila glanced back into the room. She saw nothing but an old woman she didn't know moaning incoherently.

Sheila turned toward Nurse Hill, who was still waiting. "Of course. I'm sorry. I was distracted for a moment."

Nurse Hill said nothing in reply but continued down the corridor, Sheila following behind. They came to a smaller passage to the left of the main corridor. There were four doors, and Nurse Hill stopped in front of the last one to the left, took out an enormous key ring, and unlocked the door. "Come in and have a seat, please," she said as she flipped on the lights. The room was about twelve by twelve. There were two aged folding tables and about ten folding metal chairs. Along one wall there was a sink, a refrigerator, a microwave oven, and a coffee maker. Nurse Hill pulled out a chair for Sheila, and Sheila sat down, placing her briefcase on the table. Nurse Hill walked over to the coffee maker and poured herself a cup. "Coffee, Ms. Ward?" she asked cordially.

"Yes please. Cream and sugar, if you don't mind."

Nurse Hill prepared a cup for Sheila and brought it to the table, pulled out a chair opposite Sheila, sat down, and produced a binder, placing it between herself and Sheila. After each had sipped their coffee, Sheila broke the ice. "Thank you so much for meeting me. I know you must be very busy. I just have a few questions concerning the Duvall incident, and you seem to be the only one who actually witnessed anything."

There was a pause. Nurse Hill was staring Sheila down with those pale eyes. For Sheila, who was used to dealing with people of all demeanors, it was an unusual experience to feel unnerved by someone's stare, but there was something unsettling about the experience. It was like those eyes were looking into you instead of at you. "What is your interest in this, Ms. Ward? This happened several years ago. I'm not sure what it has to do with anything you might be working on. You work with DHHS, correct?"

"Well, yes, but if you'll hear me out, I'm sure it will make sense to you."

Nurse Hill took a drink of coffee and replied, "Then by all means, give me some clarity."

Sheila cleared her throat and opened her briefcase. "As you know, Summer Duvall had a daughter the day her husband died. We received a report that raises concerns about the daughter."

"You think she's in danger, then?"

"Well, I'm not sure. And to be honest, I initially thought nothing of it."

"Nothing of it? What changed your mind?" Nurse Hill said, breaking in.

"I remembered what had happened here at the hospital all those years ago, and the name Duvall is not a common one around here, so I did some research and found out these were *the* Duvalls. This girl, Lilith Duvall, is the daughter of Danforth Duvall, who died under…strange circumstances at the time of her birth."

Nurse Hill raised her hand to pause Sheila. "I feel it is best to be exact in these situations," Nurse Hill said with the quiet authority of a woman who was accustomed to being obeyed. "First, Mr. Duvall did not die at the time of his daughter's birth. As a point of fact, he died approximately twenty-five minutes to a half hour after the birth."

Sheila nodded in assent.

"For the sake of accuracy, I have my own file concerning the incident. I thought it best that I bring it. Time can have a way of coloring memory." Nurse Hill pulled a manila folder from the binder on the table and opened it.

Sheila cleared her throat and spoke. "Not to be rude, Nurse Hill, but why would you keep a personal file on this incident?"

Nurse Hill looked at her squarely and without emotion. "Why, surely Ms. Ward, someone in your line of work can appreciate the litigious nature of the world we live in. I keep my own detailed files of all incidents outside of the norm occurring in my hospital. I do so not only for my protection, but also for the protection of the nurses who work under me. In point of fact, I began the practice very soon after becoming a nurse. I saw too many of my colleagues being thrown under the bus."

Sheila backed down. "Oh, of course. That makes sense. Besides the facts of the case…I mean, the incident, I was hoping you might give me your opinion of the nature of it."

Nurse Hill smiled. She looked more wolflike, all blue eyes and teeth. Nurse Hill pulled a photo from the file and slid it over to Sheila. The photo was of a man, or what remained of a man. He appeared to be shriveled, his skin pulled tautly across his bones. His clothes were hanging from his withered frame unscathed. The man was not burned; he was dried, desiccated. The body was curled into the fetal position on a shiny floor. His lips were drawn back from his teeth, giving the effect of a grotesque smile. Sheila shuddered a bit, and Nurse Hill noticed it.

"In your opinion, Ms. Ward, what is the nature of this man's death?"

Sheila slid the photo back to Nurse Hill, happy to be rid of it. "I don't know. That's Mr. Duvall?"

"It is. When you ask my opinion as to the nature of 'the incident,' I can only say this. I have seen a lot of death in my years as a nurse, but never anything like this. None of the doctors could give a reasonable explanation as to how a seemingly healthy man could be reduced to that state in a matter of minutes."

"Minutes?"

"Oh yes. I was there. The baby was born, no complications. Mr. Duvall asked that they be given a few moments of privacy, ostensibly to savor the moment. There was no noise, no indication that anything was going on. Mrs. Duvall rang the buzzer for a nurse. When I entered the room, I found her husband as you saw in the photo. Mrs. Duvall just held the baby, baby Lily, and sobbed. I was out of the room for no more than ten minutes."

Sheila cleared her throat. "What about the police? What did they say?"

"The police. Without knowing the cause of death, how were they to determine whether it was natural? There'd been no indication of a pathogen or a poison of any kind, and believe me, the forensics guys really tried. At the end of the day, we decided to list the death as a result of an 'unknown natural cause' and get past it. There was a good deal of fear among hospital administrators of a possible suit from Mrs. Duvall. It was decided to sweep it under the rug and pretend it never happened."

"How could there have been grounds for a suit against the hospital? I mean, if there was no cause of death determined and all that. Did the police suspect Mrs. Duvall?"

Nurse Hill took a sip of coffee and leaned across the table toward Sheila, which she found uncomfortable, but she held her position.

"I don't think you looked far enough into this, or you would know the answer. The Duvalls are an old, wealthy family. Summer, Mrs. Duvall—well, her maiden name is Bachman."

Sheila interrupted. "Bachman as in the banking family?"

"The same. No one wanted to ruffle any of those rich-connected feathers. It was easier to let it go. Mrs. Duvall wasn't raising a fuss, so they let it go."

There was a pause, a silence. The two women looked at each other across the table. Sheila, who had come here for answers, had found none. There was the issue of the little girl. Sheila had the feeling she had learned all she could. "Well, I suppose when you have a rich and powerful family, you can squirm out of anything," she said.

"You really don't know much about this, do you?" Nurse Hill asked.

"What am I missing?"

"It wasn't Mrs. Duvall's family. It wasn't the Duvalls or the Bachmans. It was Summer Duvall herself. Summer and Danforth, Mr. Duvall, were both only children. Both the sole heirs of their prospective family fortunes. I looked into it. The Duvalls were killed in a plane crash in Bolivia. Mrs. Bachman, Summer's only surviving parent, died of a heart attack. Summer Duvall, at the time of her husband's death, became the owner of all assets—both Bachman and Duvall. Literally several billion dollars."

Sheila's eyes widened despite consciously trying to maintain her composure. "My goodness!" she exclaimed. While such an outburst was second nature to her, she immediately felt self-conscious for saying it.

The Wolf looked at her with a bemused expression. "Do you want to know the strangest part of their deaths?"

Sheila nodded.

"All three died on the same day at virtually the same time."

"How is that possible? It must be a coincidence. You said the Duvalls died in South America, and I'm assuming that Mrs. Bachman was somewhere in the States."

"New Hampshire, to be exact."

"It is strange, but again, how could it be anything other than a coincidence?"

Nurse Hill shook her head. "Are you one of those people?"

"One of what people?"

"Look, I'm about as grounded in reality as most—probably more so—but over the years, I've seen too many strange things, too many instances of synchronicity, if you will, to believe in coincidence. Mr. Duvall dies in a way that is medically unexplainable. The parents die five years earlier at the same time, leaving a substantial fortune to the couple. Why does a woman who has access to a few billion dollars live in a modest home on the outskirts of a podunk town?"

Sheila was getting more and more excited. She was involuntarily tapping the rim of her coffee cup with her index finger. Nurse Hill, noticing this ideomotor movement, knew that Sheila's wheels were turning.

"What do we do?" Sheila asked.

"You mean, what do you do."

Sheila felt a bit deflated. She had hoped, perhaps felt, that Nurse Hill's interest in the case was as strong as hers. It was nice to feel like she had someone on her side for a change, especially someone like Nurse Hill.

"What I mean, Ms. Ward, is that you will have to be the one to do the legwork. You have the professional sanction to go further with this. I do not. I cannot risk my position crossing lines. This is what you do for a living. You're the investigator."

That last bit sounded like a compliment. She'd gotten few of those. She had not really thought of herself as an investigator but supposed that technically, she was.

"I feel like you need to go out to Mrs. Duvall's residence and find out what's going on out there. The girl may be in real danger. Do you think it's a coincidence that Mrs. Duvall's husband, her mother, and her in-laws are all dead?"

There was a pause. Sheila thought about the implications of what Nurse Hill was saying. If she was right, then child endangerment or abuse would be the least of Summer Duvall's crimes.

But multiple murders were not Sheila's forte. "If what you're saying is true, then shouldn't we call the police? This is way out of my depth. I mean, what do I do—just drop in and force her to confess?"

Sheila's tone of voice revealed her fear. At that moment, Nurse Hill reached across the table and took Sheila's hand. After the initial urge to pull away, Sheila felt a strange sense of calm wash over her. She hadn't felt that since her mother had passed. She looked up and saw Nurse Hill's blue eyes looking calmly at her.

"Sheila. Relax. You're not going to be alone in this. I can't go with you, but I'll be in this with you. Just stop in and do a health and welfare check. If you think you should, then recommend that the child be removed. Then we can get the police involved. We have to be careful. We can't just accuse someone like Mrs. Duvall of murder. Can you imagine the firestorm that would create? How many people know about this from your office?"

Sheila thought for a moment. "We have so many cases backlogged; they sort of pile up, you know? No one is aware of the details of the case, the connection to the deaths and all of that. To everyone else, it's one of hundreds of child welfare cases. So I guess just me, really."

"Good. Keep it that way. Go out there, and see what you can find out from her. I'll give you my cell number. If anything goes wrong, call me, and I'll be right there."

Sheila and Nurse Hill spent about an hour working out the details. Sheila felt energized. For once, she had someone in her corner. More than that, she had an adventure, a real-life mystery to solve, and maybe she would!

By now, Sheila was out of town heading through the snow-covered farm country that made up the rural areas. The snow was coming down hard, and Sheila strained to see, though the wipers were working furiously. She would have to take it slow. Part of her was very nervous about the whole thing, and left to her own devices, she would probably turn around, but she had Nurse Hill to think about. She didn't want to let her down. It was policy to let her supervisors know where she was headed on official business. The rules existed as a safety measure. DHHR employees were not always well received, and there had been incidents of violence in the past. Sheila doubted she was in any real danger, but to minimize the risk, the plan was to call Nurse Hill as soon as she arrived at the house, and ten minutes later, Nurse Hill would call her back. Sheila would tell Mrs. Duvall it was a call from her office. She and Nurse Hill had agreed the illusion would be enough to keep things civil.

Sheila had not passed another vehicle since leaving town, and it was getting dark already despite it being only 3:25 p.m. Sheila creeped along, passing picturesque farms that looked like they belonged on Christmas cards. She was getting close to the turn-off now, a gravel lane called Creek Road. Sheila slowed the car further and craned her neck, straining to see through the swirling snow. After a few minutes, she saw a green road sign reflecting her headlights. The sign was partially covered with snow, but as Sheila drew closer, she could make out the word "Creek." Sheila flipped on her left turn signal and pulled onto the gravel lane. She was surprised to see a tow truck sitting on the wide shoulder at the beginning of the road. The truck was red, and she could make out no markings on it to indicate who owned the truck. She did ascertain that the truck was idling because of the plume of vapor coming out of the exhaust pipe. Passing the truck, Sheila cruised slowly down the lane, and although the road had a few inches of snow covering its surface, she could still feel gravel under her tires. The road was more or less straight and level and passed through thick pines. The snow was heavy on the trees, and with less wind, the passage had a dreamy, peaceful feel to it. The Duvall home was only one of three on Creek Road, and the last one at that, so it would be easy to find.

A few miles in, Sheila passed a mailbox and driveway on her right and about five miles further, the next one on the left. It really was secluded. Sheila wondered how anyone could live so far removed from others. While it was true that she was an introvert, she had never been too far removed from society, at least in the periphery. Lonely, but not really alone. At last, she arrived at her destination. The Duvall house was at the very end of the road. Its driveway was at the center of a large cul-de-sac perhaps forty feet wide and was marked by two fieldstone pillars and a mailbox. Sheila stopped the car. Fumbling in her coat, she pulled out her cell phone and hit speed dial number three. Nurse Hill picked up on the third ring.

"Hello, Sheila," said Nurse Hill on the other end.

"I'm at the house." Sheila's stomach was full of butterflies.

"Are you okay?"

"Yes. A bit nervous, to be honest."

"Calm down. You've done this sort of thing a hundred times. Stick to the plan. In and out. It's 3:55. I'll call back in ten minutes like we planned. Good luck."

With that, the call ended. It felt like she had been pushed out the door of an airplane. The focus of the plan was only about fifty yards away. There was a silver Saab parked in the drive, and Sheila could see the glow of lights in the house. It was an unremarkable structure, a white box devoid of any architectural style. The main floor of the home was slightly elevated, sitting on a basement level composed of gray cinder block. As she pulled the LTD up next to the Saab, Sheila noticed small, oblong basement windows near ground level. The meter man must have seen the girl through one of these windows around the side of the house. Sheila put the transmission in park and turned off the engine. Snowflakes struck the windshield of the car as she sat for a moment and looked at the house. Sheila, out of habit, adjusted the rearview mirror and took a look at herself. She wondered absently if she should wear her hat or not, if it would make her look silly. Snapping back to reality, she decided that to wonder about her appearance at this juncture was silly enough. Grabbing her briefcase, she opened the car door and exited the car. The cold was bracing as Sheila made her way to the concrete stairs leading to a small porch at the front door. The snow was a few inches deep. and Sheila walked in short, flat, penguin-like steps to avoid slipping. As she started up the steps, the porch light burst on, startling her to the point that she let out a small squeal. She paused for a moment and continued up the last few stairs.

Standing in the open doorway, holding the storm door open with one hand, was a middle-aged woman. Her hair was long and auburn, and she was wearing a gray wool sweater and an ankle-length skirt of paisley fabric. She was attractive, tall, and slim, and in the harsh glare of the porch light, Sheila could see that the woman's eyes were green.

"My word! Get yourself in out of this cold, dear!" the woman exclaimed sweetly.

"I-I'm Sheila Ward with the DHHS."

"Very good, Sheila. Come on in before you freeze," the woman repeated, motioning her inside.

Sheila hesitated but was quickly and gently whisked into the house. This was not what Sheila had expected. In her mind, she had pictured an evil-looking shrew peering at her from a partially opened door. If this was Summer Duvall, she seemed more like an earthy, friendly hostess than a possible murderess.

Sheila found herself standing in the foyer, her hostess helping her out of her coat and admonishing her for being out on such an evening. Once things settled down, the woman turned to Sheila, held out her hand, and said, "I'm Summer Duvall. What's this all about, Sheila?"

Sheila paused, a bit disarmed after the welcome. "It's about your daughter, ma'am."

"Lily? What about her? By the way, you can call me Summer."

Sheila nodded and pushed her glasses up. The lenses were fogging. Not waiting for a response, Summer took Sheila by the elbow and walked her into the living room.

"Let me get you a tissue for those glasses, dear. Have a seat."

Sheila looked around the room. It was furnished in an eclectic, mysterious style. The room's walls were painted a soft olive green, and the hardwood floor was covered in the center of the room by a very old-looking Persian rug. On the walls, a variety of objects from masks to edged weapons to tapestries hung, some of them illuminated by sconce lighting. The effect of the room, down to the antique chair Sheila was seated on, was like stepping into a bazaar in some exotic land. The house smelled of cinnamon and other fragrant things Sheila couldn't identify. Mrs. Duvall quickly returned with a tissue and handed it to Sheila. She took a seat in a chair next to Sheila as Sheila busied herself wiping the lenses of her glasses. After checking them for clarity several times, Sheila returned them to her face. She found herself drawn to a statuette sitting on the end table to her right. The statuette was about a foot tall, beautifully carved from what looked like marble, and depicted a female figure with outstretched hands flanked on each side by deer. The woman wore a curious head-dress or hat, and her skirt was covered in small figures of bulls, goats, and other animals. The most notable features, the ones that intrigued Sheila the most, were the three rows of bulbous objects hanging about the figure's waist. Sheila looked at Mrs. Duvall, and then, pointing at the figure, she asked, "Are those breasts?"

Mrs. Duvall smiled and shook her head. "No, those are bull testicles. They were meant as offerings to the goddess. The Greeks called her Artemis, the goddess of fertility, Diana to the Romans."

"Huh," Sheila said.

Mrs. Duvall cleared her throat. "So you're here about Lily. Has there been a complaint?"

Sheila snapped back into reality and character. "Well, Mrs. Duvall—Summer—I'm not at liberty to discuss who brought the situation to our attention, of course."

"Of course," Mrs. Duvall answered.

"The concern is that your daughter may be unsupervised at times, in essence neglected."

"That is ridiculous. My daughter is very well cared for, I assure you—practically worshipped."

"That may very well be the case, but the state mandates we check on each and every reported case. I'd like to ask you a few questions, if you don't mind, and then check in on your daughter."

Mrs. Duvall smiled amiably. "Of course. I have nothing to hide. I was about to have some tea. Would you like a cup?"

"That would be nice, Mrs.—"

"Call me Summer, please," she interrupted.

"Tea would be nice, Summer."

Mrs. Duvall smiled, rose, and led Sheila to the kitchen. Like the rest of the house, the room was cozy and filled with beautiful old things. A wooden rack suspended from the ceiling over the sink held bundles of plants, some of them familiar to Sheila, like the basil, but most of them looked like they were picked from the wild. Mrs. Duvall pulled a chair out from the kitchen table. The table was made of a blond wood and was worn from use. The surface bore the patina of age but was solid. Like everything else in the place, it was most likely an antique, though Sheila really knew nothing about antiques.

Mrs. Duvall busied herself putting a kettle of water on the stove as Sheila placed her briefcase on the table, opened it, removed a paper-clipped sheaf of papers, and placed them face-down on the table. Mrs. Duvall pulled out a chair opposite Sheila and sat down, placing a wooden box and two silver tea strainers on the countertop to the right of the stove. She opened the wooden box and began to fill the strainers with a fragrant green tea. Sheila noticed the strainers were ornately carved in an intricate pattern that looked like many leaves intertwined.

Mrs. Duvall noticed Sheila was watching her intently and seemed to be drawn to the elaborate tea strainers. "They're beautiful, aren't they?"

"Yes, they are. If you don't mind me asking, are you an antique dealer?"

Mrs. Duvall smiled and shook her head. "No, not an antique dealer. I'm an anthropologist."

"Wow," said Sheila, who was not completely sure what an anthropologist did. "You have some beautiful and exotic things."

"Thank you! I've spent a lifetime collecting things from all over the world."

"You've traveled a lot?"

"Oh, yes. I love it. My husband, Danforth, and I traveled extensively. He was an archeologist. We saw so many wonderful and mysterious places."

Sheila noticed that Mrs. Duvall's voice trailed off at the end of the comment. It seemed like genuine emotion.

"You said your husband *was* an archeologist?"

Mrs. Duvall looked up from the tea for a moment, a slightly bemused look on her face. Sheila also thought she caught a glimpse of something else, maybe a look of knowing. It unnerved her a bit. At that moment, her cell phone rang, and Sheila jumped and fumbled to find her phone. After digging the phone out of her jacket pocket, she answered it.

"Sheila Ward."

From the other end, Nurse Hill spoke, "All is well with you?"

"Yes, everything is just fine here, ma'am."

"Good, see what you can get from her, but be careful. Don't push too hard."

"I'll be fine. I'll call when I leave," Sheila said, nodding thoughtfully.

"Okay, then I'll see you in a while, Ms. Ward. Bye!"

Nurse Hill ended the call.

"Is everything okay, Ms. Ward?" asked Mrs. Duvall.

"Fine. Everything is fine, thank you. The office likes to check on us when we're out."

"That must be a great comfort to you, to have someone checking in on you from time to time."

"It is."

Sheila returned her phone to her jacket pocket. Mrs. Duvall had risen from her chair and placed the tea box back into the cupboard. Sheila watched the woman intently. She seemed very calm. In Sheila's experience, most people tended to display anxiety during her visits, even those she visited with some frequency. Mrs. Duvall seemed almost indifferent to her presence, and that in itself was puzzling. Perhaps with her wealth and connection, she was unfazed by a visit from a public servant. Sheila was sure a woman like Mrs. Duvall had very good legal counsel on retainer, and the thought brought more fear. In truth, she was not following policy and procedure, and her visit, though ostensibly part of an open case, would not pass muster if put to the test. She felt her fear rising and had to tell herself to stay calm. Mrs. Duvall had placed two mugs on the table. The kettle began to whistle softly. "There we go. Nothing like a hot cup of tea on a night like this," Mrs. Duvall said, pulling the kettle from the stove and filling the cups with steaming water. The fragrance of the tea was instant and sweet, very different from anything Sheila had experienced before. Mrs. Duvall slid a cup over to Sheila. "Would you like some honey for your tea? I'm afraid I have no sugar."

Sheila nodded. "Yes, please. That would be nice."

Mrs. Duvall turned and retrieved the honey from the counter. To Sheila's surprise, it was one of those plastic bear-shaped bottles, not what she would have expected from someone who had silver tea strainers. Mrs. Duvall noticed the bemused look on Sheila's face. "Not very fancy, I know," she said, "but it sort of reminds me of when I was a kid. I just refill the bottle." Sheila chuckled out loud a bit as she took the honey and squeezed about a teaspoon into her mug. Mrs. Duvall took a seat and sipped her tea. Sheila cleared her throat. She was finding it hard not to like this woman despite the possibility she was up to something criminal.

"My husband was an archeologist," Mrs. Duvall said, nodding. "He died six years ago."

Sheila nodded, holding her mug of tea with both hands. Mrs. Duvall took a sip of tea and continued.

"He was really the most wonderful man—smart, thoughtful, totally dedicated. But I suppose we should be discussing Lily."

"I agree. You're right. Let me be clear. The allegations brought to us merely require a visit, perhaps a series of visits, to make sure she isn't in any danger. Is your daughter left alone in the home?"

"No. Of course not, as I said before. She's only six, after all. There must be some kind of misunderstanding."

"The person who brought the matter to our attention said no one answered the door and there were no cars parked in front of the house. I noticed you don't have a garage."

"I don't have a garage. I sometimes loan my car to friends and may not have heard a knock at the door. My office is at the back of the house."

"All of that sounds reasonable, and again, this is just a health and welfare visit. Do you have relatives? Your parents or maybe your husband's parents, who provide care for her when you're not able to? When you're away?"

Mrs. Duvall sat her tea on the table. "No. No grandparents. They've been dead for years, I'm afraid."

Sheila thought for a moment. While she didn't want to push too hard, she felt she had to somehow steer the conversation toward the deaths of Mrs. Duvall's husband, mother, and in-laws.

"Look, Mrs. Duvall."

"Please call me Summer."

Sheila nodded and continued. "Okay, Summer. I want to be up front with you. I'm aware that your husband's death was sudden. And somewhat..." Sheila searched her mind for the word.

"Mysterious?" Mrs. Duvall interjected.

"Mysterious, yes. I—you can probably see how the circumstances of your husband's passing might raise questions."

There was a moment of silence, awkward and heavy, but it was broken when Mrs. Duvall gave a thin smile and answered.

"Questions. What kind of questions, exactly?"

Sheila now felt squarely put on the spot. "Well, when the safety of a child comes into question, we find it important to look thoroughly into the background of the parents, or in this case, the parent. One never knows what might be important to the big picture of our investigation."

Mrs. Duvall looked as if she were deep in thought, and her eyes were fixed on Sheila's. Sheila did not detect animosity in the stare—she'd seen that many times—but this was altogether more uncomfortable. It seemed to Sheila that Mrs. Duvall's eyes were green, then blue, shifting between the two. The moment lasted only a few seconds, and then Mrs. Duvall broke the silence. "The big picture. I see. I take it you've done your homework and found my story out of the ordinary?"

"I wouldn't go as far as that. No. I think that maybe, if I may say so, the more I find out, the more questions pop up."

"Again with the questions." Mrs. Duvall picked up her cup and took a long drink of her tea. She placed the cup on the table, looked at it for a moment, and then looked up at Sheila. "Why don't you just ask?"

Sheila sat back a bit in her chair, pushed her glasses higher up on her nose and folded her hands on the table in front of her.

"I think for now it would be more productive for me to visit with your daughter for a bit, and we'll take it from there."

Mrs. Duvall pursed her lips and nodded slowly. "Okay, by all means." She pushed her chair away from the table and stood up. Sheila followed suit. Mrs. Duvall led Sheila back into the living room and then turned left into a dim hallway. About ten feet in, there was a door on the right. Mrs. Duvall opened the door, which revealed a carpeted staircase going down into the basement of the home. Mrs. Duvall started down the stairs, but Sheila paused for a moment at the top. The idea of following this woman, however benign her appearance, into the basement suddenly filled Sheila with dread. She hoped that the phone call ruse had been convincing and that Nurse Hill would not forget her. Mrs. Duvall stopped halfway down, turned, and looked up at Sheila.

"Her room is right down here, Mrs. Ward," she said, motioning her down with her hand. Sheila took the first step and kept going. At the bottom of the stairs, Mrs. Duvall turned to the right and stopped at a simple hollow-core wooden door. Sheila glanced behind them and saw that the rest of basement was unfinished. What she could see of it had an unpainted concrete floor and cinder block walls. Mrs. Duvall turned the knob and opened the door. The room was about twelve by twelve, carpeted, and the walls were painted a simple off-white. The only light came from a small lamp on the nightstand next to the single bed. Seated on the bed was a little girl wearing a blue flannel nightgown. Her waist-length hair was black, and the gloom obscured the girl's face. Sheila, her eyes trained to take in such details, noticed the absence of toys, books, or any of the other items typically found in a child's room. The only other items in the room were folding chairs leaning in the far-right corner of the room.

"We have a visitor, Lily," Mrs. Duvall said, walking past the bed. She pulled a couple of chairs from the corner, unfolded them, and set them up near the wall opposite the foot of the bed. Sheila was still standing in the doorway and found it difficult to take her eyes off the girl. There was an energy, something about the atmosphere of the room that felt odd to Sheila. The feeling was not the usual gut thing, not a hunch—it was a physical thing, like something invisible was moving around her. The girl sat on the bed, seemingly unconcerned by Sheila's presence. Through the strangeness of the sensations, her mind was cognizant of the fact that everything about this was wrong. A little girl listless, sitting in a bare room in the basement of an isolated house.

"Ms. Ward, are you okay? Please, have a seat," said Mrs. Duvall, tilting her head to one side to look Sheila in the eyes.

Sheila snapped out of it and looked at Mrs. Duvall, who motioned for her to sit. Almost against her will, Sheila complied, taking a seat on the nearest of the folding chairs. Mrs. Duvall remained standing and took a position behind and to the right of her. Sheila was feeling ill.

Sheila began to speak. "I...I'm not..."

"Shh, it's okay, Ms. Ward," whispered Mrs. Duvall.

The little girl stood up and turned to face Sheila. The girl's head tilted slightly back, and now her face was clearly visible. She was pretty, with her dark hair and pale skin, but her eyes were the most striking feature. Sheila was lost in those eyes, big and brown, seemingly bottomless pools that she found impossible to look away from. Sheila was vaguely aware that Mrs. Duvall was kneeling at her right side, whispering something to herself. Chanting. She was chanting. As Sheila was pulled deeper into the girl's gaze, a glow began to emit from around the girl, pale and green. There was an occasional crackle of what looked like electricity from the little girl's body, and Sheila's vision began to swim.

⋏

Dave was so excited. It was rare for him to be able to indulge his urges. It had become more and more difficult for him over the years to do so. The danger and consequences of being revealed had forced him to search for new avenues, avenues that were secure, discreet. As he drove, he thought about the first time his compulsion had gotten him into trouble. He had been twelve. He could still see the disgust and anger on his father's face.

"You little bastard! What the hell is wrong with you?" his father had bellowed inches from his face. "The boy's family has agreed not to go to the police. If not for my money, my position, you'd be off to some juvenile detention facility right now!"

His father had grabbed him by the neck, pushed him against the wall, and put his fist into his face. The man shook with rage.

"I won't let you destroy this family's name! Do you hear me? I won't let your disgusting perversion tear down what I've built! By God, I'll kill you, do you understand, you little piece of shit? I'll kill you before I let you!"

He had been sent to military school. His father, being well connected politically and financially, had secured a spot at venerable place in New England. He had hated it at first, before he'd realized how many opportunities were available to him. So many young boys away from home for the first time. By the time he graduated, he felt as if he had gotten the last laugh, that his father had actually rewarded him. He had learned to be stealthy, to wait, to plan. He built a solid life, a curtain of respectability and position that allowed him to fly under the radar. Experience had taught him not to leave a trail, electronic or otherwise. A chance meeting had put him on the current path. He had been suspicious at first, and it had taken a long time, the better part of year, to finally put things together. At the end, Dave had been satisfied that all was well and had taken the plunge. After a series of phone calls, cash had changed hands, and instructions had been given. His car had been left at the airport, and he had picked up the car

provided for the rest of the trip—the Mercedes he was now driving. Dave drove on through the snow. He was anxious to meet
his last contact at the end of a place called Creek Road.

Sheila felt herself drifting, like she had been sedated, and then she
was out. She felt like she was moving. Though it was dark, she
could feel air moving across her body, her face. She could hear
subtle sounds like many voices, female voices singing in a language
she did not understand. The darkness and the motion stopped,
and she found herself lying in the dirt. The place was hot and
dusty, and as she raised her head, she saw a bleak desert landscape
around her. The terrain was flat and featureless except for a hill in
the distance in front of her. It had to be a dream or a hallucination,
she told herself, but it felt very real; the rocky soil under her knees
and the dead, dry, heat felt very real. Something was here with her.
She could feel that, too. Sheila pulled herself to her feet. It was
then that she realized she was totally naked. Sheila immediately
tried to cover herself with her hands, though she still questioned
the reality of the situation. The sun was a great, red globe in the
sky pouring down its deadly heat as it settled down for the night in
the west behind the hill in the distance. Sheila saw movement to
the north and south and could see dust rising from the plain, as if
some thing or things were approaching at great speed.

"Sheila!" A cry came from a distance, from the direction of
the hill.

Sheila strained her eyes and ears to the west. The dust, and
whatever was making it, was getting closer. There was a rumble
now, low and powerful.

"Sheila! Run! Come to me!" the voice called again. The voice sounded familiar but was too faint to really make out. Sheila looked to her right and left. The rumble was louder now, and she could see black shapes moving ahead of the rising dust. Sheila raised her hand to shield her eyes from the red glow of the setting sun as she looked again to the west. Sheila began running. She ran to the west, toward the hill and the setting sun. To run was a struggle for Sheila under the best circumstances, and as she struggled ahead, rocks dug into her bare feet, but she went on in spite of them. Glancing to the right, she could clearly see the source of the dust and the roar. Bulls, great black bulls converging on her. The hill was now about two hundred yards ahead, and her pace was slow and painful.

"Sheila! Come to me! Come to us!" The voice rang loud and clear now, though she had covered little distance. Mother. It was her mother's voice.

"Mother?" Sheila sobbed, trying to keep moving forward.

The bulls were now within a hundred yards of her. Sheila stumbled on, exhausted, her feet bleeding. The bulls came on. She could feel the roar of hooves as well as hear them. Sheila looked ahead to the hill. Silhouetted against the sunset Sheila saw two forms, one of them a person, a woman Sheila was now sure was her mother. The other figure was twice as tall. The tall figure was winged like an angel, and the wings were extended, increasing the effect.

"Sheila! Join us!" her mother cried.

Sheila stumbled on, closer to the hill. Her strength was waning, and she was sure she would be run down by the herds closing in on her from both sides of the path to the hill. The bulls were too close, the distance too far. In despair, Sheila cried out.

"Help me, Mother! I can't make it! Please help me!"

Sheila had come to a stop. She looked ahead at the figures on the hill. The tall winged figure raised its arms. The bulls, only a few feet away, stopped in their tracks. The great beasts stood in line on either side of the path, panting and heaving. The dust from their charge swept forward, momentarily obscuring Sheila's view of the hill. When it cleared, Sheila could again see her mother and the winged figure clearly.

"Mother," Sheila sobbed, dropping to her knees.

"Rise!" A voice thundered. It was not the voice of her mother but someone or something else. The voice seemed to come from all around her, yet she knew the winged figure was the source. Sheila looked up. A green aura flickered around the figure. Lightning crackled through the red sky.

"Rise and come home," the voice called out.

Sheila felt a calm wash over her. All of her pain, doubt, and fear melted away. She stood without effort and began to walk. The bulls, lined up on either side of the path, had lowered their heads as if in submission. Sheila could feel their hot breath, still labored from their exertions, on her as she passed.

"Do you come of your own will? A free woman?" The figure asked serenely.

"I do," Sheila answered.

"Anointed are the daughters of Lilith," the voice answered. The figure then dropped her arms quickly.

The effect was as if all of the bulls had been simultaneously decapitated by invisible blades, their heads falling from their bodies. Blood sprayed from their necks, bathing Sheila's body. By the time she was past the last of the slaughtered bulls and starting up the hill, she had been showered head to toe. Sheila began to ascend the hill. The blood was thick and sticky on her body, and by this time, she was close enough to see her mother clearly. She looked strong and vibrant and was wearing a long robe of white. The tall, winged figure was female with skin the color of bronze, and Sheila found it impossible to look away from the figure's eyes. They were large in proportion to the stature of the winged figure and were brown, soft and inviting like the eyes of a deer. Sheila was near the top, her mother waiting with open arms. While Sheila was aware of her mother's presence, she kept her eyes fixed on the winged figure's eyes. As she stepped in front of her mother and the winged being, Sheila was looking nearly straight up into those deep, soft brown eyes. Sheila's mother stepped forward, embraced her, and then guided her back, closer to the figure. Sheila saw the eyes turn a bright green, and then she was enveloped by darkness as the figure's wings folded around her and her mother.

"Sheila."

"Sheila, wake up."

Sheila stirred and opened her eyes. She found herself lying on a cold, vinyl floor looking up at Mrs. Duvall, who was looking down at her with a kindly look on her face.

"Where am I?" Sheila muttered, "What happened?"

"You did well, Sheila. We thought you would."

Mrs. Duvall offered Sheila her hand. Sheila took it and got to her feet. After steadying herself against the sink, Sheila realized she was naked. She was also covered with dried blood. Her literal mind grasped what her subconscious mind already knew—it had not been a dream. What was happening—the winged figure, her mother, the bulls—it was all real. With this realization, Sheila also felt something else, something she had never really felt—an inner calm, a peace. And Sheila felt strong.

Mrs. Duvall motioned to the shower. "There are towels and washcloths for you. Get cleaned up, hon. I'll bring you a robe. I took the liberty of washing your clothes. They'll be done in a bit. Come out when you're finished, and we'll talk. Would you like some more tea?"

"Please," Sheila said. Her mind wondered why she felt no shame at her nakedness, how she could possibly be at peace, and most of all, how she could accept what had just happened.

Mrs. Duvall nodded and left the bathroom, closing the door behind her. Sheila pulled back the shower curtain, turned on the water, tested the temperature, and stepped in. Her skin, which had felt tight from the dried blood, felt immediately slippery as the hot water hit it, and as the blood dissolved and ran off of her body, Sheila felt clean, new. After showering and toweling off, Sheila put on the bathrobe Mrs. Duvall had left her. Sheila opened the door and walked down the hallway, pausing for a moment at the basement door. For reasons she didn't understand, Sheila put her hand on the door, almost as homage to the force in the basement. After a few moments, moments that felt strangely like worship, Sheila crossed through the living room to the kitchen where Mrs. Duvall was busy preparing two mugs of tea.

"Sheila. You are most welcome," said Mrs. Duvall, turning to her and embracing her.

Sheila, in a flood of emotion, burst into tears, sobbing on Mrs. Duvall's shoulder. Mrs. Duvall shushed her, stroking her wet hair. In a few minutes, Sheila was okay. She straightened herself and gently pulled away from Mrs. Duvall.

"How? What?" Sheila stammered.

"Sit down, Sheila." Mrs. Duvall said, motioning to the table. "I know you have many questions. You're not afraid anymore, are you?"

Sheila knew exactly what Mrs. Duvall was talking about. She had felt fearful since as far back as she could remember—afraid of being seen, afraid of life. But she didn't feel any fear now. Sheila pulled out a chair and took a seat opposite Mrs. Duvall.

"I am not afraid, Mrs. Duvall, not of anything. I…I'm so happy." Sheila stopped, a look of confused tranquility on her face.

"Good. Good for you," said Mrs. Duvall. "You are part of something now, bound to it, bound to the goddess."

"Lily?"

"No. Lily is the vessel."

"The vessel? I don't understand."

Mrs. Duvall nodded, and Sheila saw a gleam in the woman's green eyes.

"Listen, then, and remember. This is our creation story. It began when my husband and I met in college. In truth, Danforth and I often speculated that the wheels of our destinies had begun to turn long before we met, that as nothing in this world occurs by chance, it stands to reason that we had been born for this one purpose."

"What purpose?" Sheila interrupted.

"Listen, Sheila. We haven't a lot of time right now."

Sheila nodded in assent, clutching her mug closer to her, looking like a child listening to a bedtime story.

"The purpose, Sheila, is to bring the goddess back into this realm, this reality," Mrs. Duvall continued.

"The goddess Lilith, or Ninlil, goddess of the grain, of the open field, of the south wind. They were all deposed as the belief of mortals shifted to the one God. Without sacrifice and worship, they faded into the other realm. Danforth and I shared an interest in the religions of the ancients, and we got a chance many years ago to travel to Nuffar, Iraq, as part of a team of archeologists and anthropologists doing further excavations near the temple complex there. We were only volunteers at that time, you understand. Just part of a larger group of students who did the tedious work of such an endeavor. One night I had a dream, and in the dream, I was shown a cave, or more correctly, where to find the cave. I spoke to Danforth about it, and he revealed to me he'd experienced a similar dream. When the dig was complete, we decided to stay in Iraq. We had money even then. As you well know, we both come from wealthy families. The right excuses were made, and in any case, we began to seek out the site of the cave. This was before the war with Iran, and as long as one had the means, it was fairly easy for Westerners to move about. Saddam was buying weapons for his planned war against Iran, and for the right price, you could dig and take what you wished. What we found was astonishing. The cave was the entrance to an underground temple complex devoted to Lilith. This was the summer of 1980. We decided to have everything moved to the States. War was looming, and we knew that once it started, we would never get anything out. But we did get everything out. While we worked to decipher it all—the clay tablets, the inscriptions on the walls and statuary—we continued studying all aspects of the occult and found like-minded people who could help us learn. After school, we planned on marriage. Our families were all for it, but they wanted a traditional church ceremony. They were upset that we didn't want that, and when we expressed a bit of our beliefs, they were rabidly opposed to the union. There were threats that we would be cut off, written out of the wills. We relented and made nice with them, allowing them to think that all was well. You know all three of them died on the same day, don't you?"

Sheila nodded, looking over her mug. "Um-hmm."

"Of course, you do," Sheila continued. "You're a smart woman, and you've done your homework, or you wouldn't be here. We had to wait until the time was right. In this case, the summer solstice was when our powers would be amplified. We cast our spell. It took us twelve hours of chanting the incantations, more than that to prepare, but the results speak for themselves, don't they? My mother died from a medical condition, and Danforth's parents were killed in an airplane crash. No investigation, no need for one. Our inheritances were secure. Our parents were out of the way. We could marry as we saw fit, and more importantly, we had a vast fortune with which to further our studies and cause. The Preservation Society helped a great deal, and not just us. There are many individuals and groups out there. You'll see. With our financial needs secure, we were free to finally grasp the relevance of what we had found in Iraq. The goddess could be brought back! None of what we had been taught was true. The stories of gods and goddesses weren't myths. They were real but diminished. The tablets revealed to us the ceremony that would start to bring the goddess back. Danforth and I performed the ritual at the appointed time in our union. We created a vessel in which the goddess could return to this plane."

"Lily!" Sheila exclaimed.

Mrs. Duvall nodded. "Yes. It was Lily. The product of our ritual. Lilith resides in her. Danforth gave himself as a willing sacrifice at her birth. The first had to be a willing sacrifice. He gave his life force, his aura, to her."

Sheila had an astonished look on her face. The mystery of Danforth Duvall's death was solved. There was a look of genuine sadness on Mrs. Duvall's face.

"I'm sorry, Summer, so sorry," Sheila said, placing her mug on the table and taking Mrs. Duvall's hands in hers.

Mrs. Duvall smiled tenderly and squeezed Sheila's hands. "Thank you. You're a dear. Danforth knew the sacrifice he would have to make. When Lily becomes a woman, comes of age, Lilith will take her place on earth once more. She will regain her spiritual form and power and be able to manifest herself physically. A new age. A religious Renaissance. The power of the patrician broken. In the mean time, we care for Lily; we nurture and feed the goddess."

"What will become of Lily after the goddess is restored?" Sheila asked, wide-eyed.

"Lily will go on a demigoddess. She will be the high priestess of our religion, venerated, the mother of Lilith, but also a daughter."

Sheila turned quickly in her chair as if something had startled her. She stood up and walked to the sink. Sheila parted the curtain of the window above it and peered into the night as if she expected something.

"The Wolf is coming," Sheila said, still peering out the window.

"The Wolf?" Mrs. Duvall asked.

"Nurse Hill. The Wolf. She is one of us, too."

Mrs. Duvall smiled, looking pleased. "Yes. She is coming. I like that—the Wolf. She was an early convert and is quite an asset. She was there at the beginning. You seem to have many gifts, Sheila. Nurse Hill said you were special. Well, there's plenty of time to learn more later. We'd better go downstairs. We have company, dear."

Sheila nodded and turned away from the window. The story she had just heard, the experience she was having, the things she knew she would be asked to do—she questioned none of it. She had been initiated, anointed. She had a knowing that transcended doubt. Sheila followed Mrs. Duvall downstairs to the basement. Lily was sitting on her bed, her hair obscuring her face. Sheila felt as if there were electricity flowing through her body as she passed the girl. Mrs. Duvall set up two of the folding chairs and placed them against the wall opposite Lily's bed.

"Please sit, Sheila," said Mrs. Duvall, motioning to the chairs. Sheila sat down and was followed by Mrs. Duvall. Once they were seated, Mrs. Duvall took Sheila's hand, gave it a gentle squeeze, and looked her in the eyes.

"The goddess must feed. There must be a sacrifice."

Sheila nodded. Lily sat on the edge of the bed, upright, her gaze falling on Sheila. Sheila, instead of squirming and looking away as she normally would have, looked straight into the girl's eyes. Beyond the dark, soft pools, Sheila saw flashes of something more. Flashes of other times and places ancient and sacred. And then there was something earlier, deepest of all, glimpses of the birthplace of the old gods, fantastic and surreal. Sheila was lost in the sights and sounds when Summer tugged at her shirtsleeve.

"Come back, dear," she said, smiling. "No time to travel right now."

"Oh, sorry. I—" Sheila began, but Summer squeezed her hand again.

"We'll work on it later. Don't worry, Sheila; he'll only see what she wants him to see. He'll never notice us."

Sheila had not really worried about whether or not they would be seen. Sheila was still reeling. Everything she thought she knew was gone forever—reality, her identity. She felt as if a dam had been broken within her mind and spirit. All of the doubt she might have felt, perhaps *should* have felt, simply wasn't there. For the first time, she knew the meaning of faith. She had faith in Lilith, in her sisters, and in herself. With real faith there was no room for fear or doubt, and she would accept her role, whatever it might be. She heard the door at the top of the stairs open and the sound of a man and a woman conversing playfully. The woman was the Wolf. It was Nurse Hill. The man's voice had an excited, almost crooning quality. Sheila could hear them descending the staircase, and then the bedroom door opened.

"This way, Dave," said Nurse Hill, holding the door open for him.

The man was well dressed and middle aged, and he wore a wedding band. It was obvious to Sheila that the man was very excited. As he entered the room and saw Lily, he let out a low whistle.

"You were right, sweetie," he said, turning to Nurse Hill. "She's just right. Love those shy ones."

Nurse Hill smiled and nodded in affirmation. She looked stunning, almost like a different person. She was wearing a blue dress, and her hair and makeup were immaculate. Sheila could think of only one word to describe her—sexy.

"Maybe when I'm finished here, you and I can play," the man said, putting his hand on Nurse Hill's hip.

"One thing at a time, David," Nurse Hill replied, smiling. Her blue wolf-eyes flashed. Sheila looked at Mrs. Duvall and smiled. Again, she squeezed Sheila's hand.

Dave turned away from Nurse Hill, nodding. He stepped into the room and pulled the door closed behind him.

"Hey, sweetie. You sure are a pretty one," he said, stepping toward Lily. "Don't be afraid, honey. Let's see those eyes."

Lily looked up, her dark eyes staring at him.

Sheila could hear a low, whining moan coming from Dave. His body was quaking gently.

Lily stood and took a step closer to him, her eyes black and menacing.

Dave was now emitting a stifled scream, his body shaking harder.

Lily extended her arms, the palms of her hands upright as if she were in a state of peaceful meditation. A dull, green glow was emanating from her eyes, moving toward Dave. As it reached him, his body convulsed and was lifted a few inches from the floor. He was levitating, contorted and screaming.

Lily stood in a pose of complete serenity. Sheila could feel the power pulsing through the room, a series of waves flashing over her, through her.

Dave's body was desiccating, shriveling. The mystery of Danforth Duvall's death was now solved. It was over in a moment. The light faded, and Lily lowered her arms. Dave's remains fell to the floor. He sounded dry and hollow, like a dried gourd or a piñata.

The aftermath was anticlimactic, like a small cleanup on aisle five. Dave's remains were taken to the other side of the basement, broken up and fed into the wood stove. The three women adjourned to the kitchen for some tea and sandwiches, prepared by their gracious host, Mrs. Duvall. While they ate and chatted, the tow truck Sheila had seen at the end of the road arrived to collect the loaner Mercedes Dave had driven to the house. The truck was, of course, driven by another sister, another of Lilith's daughters.

"I'm so glad you made it. I knew you would," said Nurse Hill to Sheila, taking her hand firmly. Sheila teared up, and Summer uttered an "Oh my!" and took both of their hands in hers. In that moment, Sheila realized she would never be afraid or lonely or lost again. She had sisters, many of them, and she had a purpose. They had a purpose. Together they would bring a goddess back from across the void. They would upset the world, bring it back into balance. Sheila felt very fortunate indeed.

DOUBLE FEATURE IN PURGATORY

"**D**amn!" Ronald exclaimed as his phone dropped the call. He took his eyes off the road and glanced at the phone's screen. Seeing that he had no bars, he tossed the phone onto the passenger seat in disgust. The car's headlights peered into the darkness as he drove north on I-79. He was somewhere in West Virginia, north of Charleston. This stretch of interstate was a series of curves and hills carved into the mountains, with hardwood forest on both sides. The forest was broken up only occasionally by a home or a farm. Ronald was so tired. Not just physically, but emotionally. His wife, Eliza, had just called with more bad news. There never seemed to be enough money since losing his job a couple of years ago. He had been trying, really trying, to make things happen with his new job as a salesman, but it appeared he may not have the touch, so again his wife had called him with that hesitant worry in her voice.

The bank had called, she said. "I know you're trying, hon, but they said we're late again. I really need to go grocery shopping. We're out of everything."

Ronald hated the fact that he could not adequately provide for his family, hated to hear that his wife had to worry about simply buying food. It was one thing after another these days. If it were not for the love he had for his wife and children, he would have given up long ago, would have let the house and cars go, let it all go, and would have just walked away. At forty-three, he had imagined by now things would be set, that he would be looking forward to a stable life into his retirement. But as it turned out, there was nothing but more uncertainty.

The highway passed under his wheels as he continued north toward home. He was starting to get a headache, and the worry didn't help. The trip had not been a total loss. He'd made a few sales, and his commission would be enough to cover things for now. He told himself that he just had to keep going, to not give up. A spark of hope remained, and after all, it had been darker for him a year ago. He had gotten so low, so depressed, that he had considered suicide. He had even planned to make it look like an accident so Eliza and the kids would get the life insurance money. With double indemnity, they would get $250,000—enough to pay off the house and cars and still have plenty left to live on for a while. But in the end, he couldn't bring himself to do it. The love of his wife and two children had carried him through his depression. He could not bear the thought of his children growing up fatherless, his wife suffering the pain that his suicide would bring her. On a more selfish note, he loved them so much he couldn't be without them. He fought through it. He would slug it out. Maybe he could find some more work on the side somewhere. It was about ten o'clock, and Ronald figured that with one more stop to fuel up, get some coffee, and stretch his legs, he would be home by about one in the morning. The kids would be asleep, but Eliza would be up waiting for him as she always was. He missed them so much when he was away, and it seemed these days, he was always trying to get back to them, to get home. An all-consuming cycle was in play—chase the money, do what he had to do to make ends meet, and then find his way back to them.

Ronald's head was pounding. He reached for the glove box latch, keeping his eyes on the road. He pulled the latch, and the glove box fell open. Feeling along the inside of the glove box, he found what he was looking for, a small plastic bottle of ibuprofen. Being the considerate and loving person she was, Eliza always made sure he had little things like this in his car. Ronald brought the bottle up to his mouth, and using his teeth, he popped the cap off of the bottle, letting it fall to the floorboard. Ronald let a couple of tablets roll into his mouth and swallowed them. He transferred the bottle to his left hand, which was still holding the steering wheel. Meanwhile, he reached forward with his right hand, groping around under the seat, looking for the errant cap. At that moment, his cell phone rang. Ronald abandoned the search for the bottle cap and reached for his phone on the passenger seat. Ronald took his eyes off the highway and picked up his phone. He could see that it was his wife calling him back. Ronald looked up from the phone to the road ahead. Deer. Ronald braked hard and cut the wheel to the right. The car was skidding and spun out of control. Ronald was unsure which way his car was going. There was the sound of gravel and a loud bang.

Then there was silence. The car had somehow ended up on the shoulder, facing north, surrounded by a cloud of dust. Ronald had a death grip on the steering wheel, and his body was violently trembling. With some difficulty, he pulled his hands from the steering wheel and undid his seatbelt. The dust had almost dissipated when he opened the door and stepped out of the car to survey the damage. Ronald started at the front of the car and was amazed that there was none whatsoever. Ronald made it to the rear of the car before a wave of nausea overtook him and he had to vomit. He leaned against the car for a long time, letting his nerves settle, and then went around and got back in, put on his seatbelt, and started the car up. Placing the car in drive, he was amazed at his luck. He'd thought he was a goner back there. He felt like the car had flipped. Still very shaken, he kept his speed at about fifty. Just ahead, Ronald could see an exit on the right. Flipping on his turn signal, Ronald eased onto the exit ramp. At the bottom of the exit ramp, there was a two-lane secondary road going to the right. Ronald stopped the car. He could see no signs, no gas stations, no convenience stores. The area looked uninhabited, just patches of woods and farmland. Over a slight rise in the terrain to his right, however, Ronald could make out the glow of lights above the tree line. The glow was definitely something more than a farm or home, maybe a gas station or truck stop. Ronald paused a moment longer. Maybe he should get back on the highway. But how? He had seen no signs indicating a way to return to the interstate. Maybe farther down this route, there would be a way back. Seemingly without thinking, Ronald eased off the brake and started smoothly down the road. The road was flanked on either side by wire fencing, and the land was typical broken farmland consisting of fields interspersed with woodlots. After about half a mile, the road made a turn to the left and then started up a rise. At this point, the area was more heavily wooded, and there were no structures to be seen, but the soft glow still beckoned ahead.

The car broke over the top of the rise, and there it was: the source of the glow. About a quarter of a mile ahead and to the right, Ronald could see an illuminated screen.

"A drive-in?" Ronald muttered to himself.

Ronald thought all the drive-ins were shut down. With the steady drumbeat of technology—VHS, DVD, and now streaming content—drive-ins had steadily closed. The more recent move to digital format as opposed to the traditional thirty-five-millimeter film had been the final nail in their coffin, or so he'd thought. Ronald started down the other side of the rise. As he got within about five hundred feet of the drive-in, Ronald slowed the car, pulled it onto the gravel shoulder, and stopped. Putting the car in park but leaving the engine running, Ronald sat there for a moment, looking ahead at the inviting glow of the giant outdoor screen. He needed to get back onto the highway, he thought, but as he looked ahead, his mind was full of nostalgia. He had spent so many Friday and Saturday nights during his youth and young adulthood at places just like this. Ronald opened his door and stepped out of the car. Walking to the front of the car, Ronald took it all in. He could hear the sound carrying in the night air, the sound of whatever was playing, hard to make out, and the sound of crickets behind that. The air was cool, and he could smell fresh-cut hay like perfume in the air. Ronald closed his eyes, took a deep breath, and exhaled slowly, feeling a sense of calm. Ronald got back into his car, put it in gear, and drove up to the entrance. Making a right onto the gravel entry, he saw a large sign on his left lit all around its edges by light bulbs that read simply Twilight Drive-In and "Open Fri–Sat nights: $5 adults, $3 kids." Below that, in big, black, plastic letters, it read "Now Showing *The Thing* and *Halloween.*"

Ronald was a huge John Carpenter fan, and he was pleasantly surprised that these two movies were playing. Maybe it was one of those retro movie nights or something. He had made up his mind, perhaps unconsciously, that he was going in. As the car rolled forward toward the cinder block ticket booth, Ronald suddenly remembered his wife and kids. He had to get home, didn't he? Again, he stopped the car and put it in park. Glancing up at his rearview mirror to make sure he wasn't holding anyone up, he then turned on his dome light. Where was his phone? Ronald, not finding it on the seat next to him, unbuckled his seat belt and leaned over to the passenger side, feeling around under the seat. After a few moments of groping, he felt his phone. Turning it on, he was relieved that he had a bar of service. Ronald dialed his home number, and after five rings, it went to voicemail: "This is the Clarks. We're not in right now, but leave us a message after the beep. Thanks."

"They must be in bed already," Ronald thought. There was the beep. "Hey, sweetie. It's Ronald. I hope you and the kids are doing okay. I'm on my way, so don't worry. Guess what I just found? A drive-in! Can you believe it? Anyway, I'm going to check it out, maybe get a cup of coffee. I could use a little break. I won't stay long. If it looks good, maybe we can bring the kids some time. Remember how we used to love it? Okay, then. I'll call you when I get back on the highway. Love you all so much. Bye."

Ronald hung up, put his phone back on the passenger seat, and put the car in gear. As he approached the ticket booth, he noticed there was a corrugated-metal fence about eight feet high to his right, and it looked like it must border the whole place. The booth was painted white and had a metal roof that ran about twelve feet on either side of the building, forming a tollbooth-like structure for the entrance and exit of cars. It was just like every other drive-in he had ever been to. Stopping at the ticket window, he was greeted by an older man with gray hair; he was thin and was smoking an enormous cigar. "Welcome to the Twilight, sir!" he said, smiling. "How many?"

"Just me, sir," Ronald replied. "One adult, please."

"That will be five dollars, sir," the man replied through a cloud of cigar smoke.

"I don't think I have any cash, sir. Do you take debit cards?"

"Sorry, sir. We do not," the man replied, smiling broadly. "Surely you have five dollars?"

Ronald pulled out his wallet, turned on the dome light, and took a look. In his wallet was a crisp new twenty. "Must have forgotten about that." Ronald said, pulling the bill out and handing it to the man.

"All righty! One adult, and fifteen dollars is your change, sir. And here's one of our flyers. You can use the speakers or tune your radio to 98.5 FM," said the man, handing Ronald his change and a small flyer printed on lime-green paper.

"Thanks," Ronald said, putting his car into gear and pulling ahead. The layout was typical of a classic drive-in, with the concessions building sitting roughly in the center of lot. The cinder block structure was white and doubled as the projector room, an intense beam of light emanating from the arc-lamp projector housed in a room at the front of the structure. Rows of steel speaker posts, again painted white like everything else, marked the lanes. Ronald picked a lane near the middle and proceeded slowly between the already parked cars. Ronald saw a beautiful late-sixties Pontiac GTO, several older pickup trucks, and a station wagon. The station wagon was backed into its space with the back open, and he could see a pile of kids in the back lying on blankets and watching the movie. It reminded him so much of his own childhood. Summer breaks, his parents took him and his brothers almost every weekend. Ronald found an empty spot to the right side behind the concessions building and eased in until he was within easy reach of his speaker. Once satisfied with his spot, Ronald rolled his window down and shut off the car.

"No radio for me. I'm going old school," Ronald said aloud to himself, lifting the aluminum speaker off the post and hanging it from the inside of his car door. The sound was weak, so Ronald adjusted the black plastic knob to the right, increasing the volume. As he did this, the speaker crackled a bit but settled down once the adjustment was finished. Ronald settled back, adjusting his seat, and took in the atmosphere of this place. In front of him, before the huge screen that he could see was faced with white-painted corrugated metal if he looked closely, were rows of cars, people sometimes walking between them toward the concession building. Though he'd seen it so many times, Ronald lost himself in the movie—Kurt Russell playing the reluctant hero trying to save the Antarctic outpost, and later the world, from a shape-shifting alien invader picking off his companions one by one.

Near the end of the movie, a thought crossed Ronald's mind. Wasn't there someplace he had to be? He tried hard to remember but couldn't, so he went back to the movie. As the breeze shifted, Ronald picked up the smell of popcorn, coffee, and maybe hot dogs. He was pretty hungry, and the movie was almost over, so Ronald decided to beat the rush to the concession stand. Replacing the speaker on its pedestal, Ronald opened his door and walked behind the cars in his row toward the concession building. As he walked past the cars and trucks, almost all of them old models, he saw a mixture of people: a young couple (probably teenagers making out), several families, and a few single patrons like himself. As he approached the concession building, he could smell the fresh-cut hay from the fields bordering the drive-in, popcorn, and coffee, and he could hear the crickets singing behind the sound of the movie. At the concession building entrance, mayflies and moths danced around beneath the fluorescent lights above the glass-and-aluminum door.

A large sign on the door read PUSH, so he pushed and swung the door open. It was warm inside the building, the whole thing lit with slightly buzzing fluorescent ceiling lights. The floor was covered in old, well-worn vinyl that had probably once had a pattern of some sort on it. At the two entrances, the flooring was worn white and held down with old-fashioned carpet tacks. To his left was the snack bar. Signs, some handwritten and some printed, advertised popcorn, various candies, hot dogs (with chili or slaw if you liked), burgers, pizza, and pretzels. Both soft drinks and coffee were offered. To Ronald's right, a short hall had bathrooms, men on the right and women on the left, and at the end of the hallway through an open door, Ronald could see the projector. Out of curiosity, Ronald walked to the projection room doorway and peeked inside. The projector was an enormous old thing, all brass and steel with a chimney of galvanized pipe going to the ceiling to vent heat. Between the projector and the large steel-topped horizontal film table to the left of it, a rotund older woman was leaning, smoking a cigarette. Noticing Ronald's curiosity, she smiled at him, exhaled some smoke, and said, "How are you this evening, sir?"

Ronald noticed a large strawberry-colored birthmark on the woman's left cheek. Her auburn hair was up in a loose bun on her head, and she wore a pink blouse with a kitten embroidered on the left pocket.

"I'm fine, ma'am. How are you doing tonight?" Ronald said, smiling.

"Hot. Hot is how I am, sir," she said, giggling a bit. "This old beast really puts off the heat. That and the snack bar."

"I bet," Ronald said, smiling and nodding. "That's quite a projector you have there. Thirty-five millimeter?"

The woman nodded.

"Original to this drive-in?" Ronald asked.

"No. No it's not. This is our second projector. Tom bought it used, mind you, but it's better than the old one. This is a 1957 model, I think."

The woman leaned toward the doorway and yelled in the direction of the snack bar, "This projector's a '57 model, right, Tom?"

Ronald looked toward the snack bar. An old man with close-cropped white hair and glasses leaned over the counter and answered her. "That's right, Irma, that one's a 1957 model."

Irma nodded and smiled. "I thought so, sir. 1957. Sorry about the yelling. Old Tom's a bit hard of hearing."

"That's okay," Ronald said. "So you guys don't have a digital projector? I thought everyone had switched over."

"Not us. No, sir, not us. If it ain't broke, don't fix it, I say. I've heard of the digital ones from other folks, too, but some things are better if they don't change, you know?"

"Absolutely. I agree. This place is perfect. Reminds me of when I was young. Probably my favorite place in the world, truth be known. A drive-in."

"That's why you're here, I bet," Irma said, smiling sweetly and knowingly. "You're going to just love your time here, sir. Everyone does, you know."

Ronald nodded in agreement but felt a little confused by Irma's last statements. "Well, Irma, thanks for the tour and info. I'm going to grab some food and coffee before the rush. Name's Ronald, by the way."

Irma returned her cigarette to her lips and clasped Ronald's hand in both of hers. "Pleased to meet you, Ronald. Come back and see me anytime. I'll show you how this beauty works."

"I'll do that, Irma." Ronald broke Irma's grasp and backed away. "Thanks so much! Have a good evening."

Ronald turned and walked to the concession stand. As he stood perusing the menu, the old man, Tom, approached the counter and smiled broadly.

"What can I get for you, young man?" Tom asked.

Ronald looked over the offerings on the board behind Tom for a moment and said, "How about one chili dog, a small popcorn, and a medium coffee?"

"Coming right up, sir," Tom replied, turning to fill the order.

As Ronald waited for his food, he marveled at how this place was truly a time capsule. Everything from the speakers and screen to the concession stand looked as if it had remained unchanged. Ronald looked hard behind the counter, watching the old man work, and could not even see a microwave oven back there. From a door behind the food prep area, a petite old woman emerged carrying what looked like a batch of fresh cole slaw.

"Gotta beat that rush, Tom. Movie's almost over," she said.

"Let me help you with that, sweetie," Tom said, taking the container from her hands and planting a little kiss on her forehead.

"Always my hero, hon," the old woman said, offering a smile and a nod to Ronald.

Ronald returned the gesture. How adorable the two of them were! Tom finished his order and placed it on the counter. Everything was hot and fresh and smelled delicious. Ronald was hungrier than he'd thought.

"Let's see. Hot dog with chili, small popcorn, and a medium coffee," Tom said, writing the order on a small pad. Without looking up, he added, "Cream and sugar and napkins are over to the right. Help yourself, sir. That will be five dollars, please."

Ronald pulled out his wallet and opened it. Instead of the three fives he had received in change at the ticket booth, there again was a single crisp twenty. Ronald had a brief moment of confusion, but he let it go. He produced the twenty and handed it to Tom.

"Out of a twenty, and fifteen is your change, sir," Tom said, producing the bills from a small metal box he'd retrieved from under the counter.

"Thanks so much, sir. Thought I would get in here before the movie ends," Ronald said, putting his change in his wallet.

"A wise move, sir. Gets pretty busy between movies. I think the fresh air makes people hungry. Trade secret, though," Tom said, winking at Ronald.

Ronald smiled and answered, "Seems to have worked on me."

Tom chuckled and put the money box back under the counter.

"No register?" Ronald asked offhandedly.

"Never needed one, friend," Tom said pleasantly. "Pretty good folks here. Never any problems. Not really about the money anyway, I guess. I got lucky. Been here a long time, and it's really been everything I ever needed or wanted. How would you put it? I am content." The last part Tom finished with a flourish of his right hand, the kind of thing one might see in an old movie. Ronald found it very charming.

"How long have you been working here, if you don't mind me asking?" Ronald inquired.

Tom put his elbow on the counter and rested his chin in his hand, looking a bit like *The Thinker*.

"It's easier for me these days to tell you when I started." Tom smiled and continued. "Dr. Brown built this place in 1948. The summer of '48, mind you. I worked here the following summer and the summer after that, and so on. Started out parking cars."

"Parking cars?" Ronald asked, a quizzical look on his face.

"Well, you have to remember that things were pretty different back then," Tom said, placing another elbow on the counter and hand under his chin. His blue eyes were sparkling as he spoke. "Very few folks had TV back then, and the theaters were only in the bigger towns, so for most part, we were it if you wanted to catch a show. This place ran five or six days a week during the summer in the early days, weather permitting of course."

Ronald nodded.

"So we could get everyone a spot, several of us local boys parked cars. Didn't actually park them, mind you; that's just what we called it. One of us would meet you at the ticket booth, and we'd guide you with a flashlight to your spot till we were full. Sometimes we had to turn folks away. It was a big deal back then, you know."

"Wow! I had no idea," Ronald said, really interested. He thought he knew all there was to know about drive-ins, having spent a great deal of time in them in the seventies and eighties.

"So you've been here since 1948?" Ronald asked, his eyes wide.

Tom shook his head. "Not exactly, sir."

Ronald interrupted him. "Please, call me Ronald."

Tom extended his right hand, and the two men shook on it.

"Pleased to meet you, Ronald," Tom said. "Please call me Tom."

Tom put his chin back in his hands and continued. "You see, Ronald, I got drafted in 1950 and ended up in Korea in '51. I was on a Sherman tank. Really felt invincible until a T-34 rung our bell. It was a bad year for us over there. I was the only one who made it home out of our crew. Spent about a year in a hospital in Japan recuperating."

Ronald was shaking his head thoughtfully "I'm sorry to hear you had such a rough time. Thanks for your service."

Tom smiled and shook his head. "No need to thank me, Ronald; we all pretty much served back then. So those two years I wasn't here, but when I got back home, I enrolled in college. We had the GI bill, you know; got a degree in mechanical engineering. All through school, I worked here each summer. Met my wife here, too. She was a carhop, you know, prettiest one here." Tom gave a sly smile and wink.

Ronald nodded and smiled goofily in spite of himself.

"So you could say I spent my life here. Made my life here. All of our children worked here in the summers, too. I could do most of my engineering work, drawings and things, from home, so we were always together. Anyway, that's my story, the story of this place. A lot has changed over the years, movies and things, cars...you know. But at its core, this place and places like it are kind of magical. I guess that's what brings people here, what keeps them."

Ronald nodded. He knew what Tom meant. In the back of his mind, he thought that he had to go somewhere, be with someone, but it was only a shadow in his mind. In this place, he felt at ease. This felt like home.

"Tom, you, sir, are a fortunate man. A life well lived," Ronald said, shaking Tom's hand again.

"I did live that life well," Tom said with an extra squeeze of Ronald's hand.

People had started to filter into the concession building, and with that, Ronald gathered his food and headed out past them. A tall, lanky young man, maybe eighteen or nineteen, with long blond hair and wearing an AC/DC T-shirt, held the door open for him. Once outside, Ronald passed two young women wearing miniskirts, their hair in tall beehives. As he walked to his car, some things were working their way around his head. What had Irma said? "That's why you're here, I bet" and "You'll love your time here. Everyone does." And Tom: "I did live that life well." Before he could ruminate on it very much, he had reached his car. Ronald hopped inside, turned on the dome light, and placed his food on the seat next to him and his coffee in the cup holder. As he placed his food on the seat, he found a small, dark plastic object about the size of a pack of cigarettes. Ronald was truly puzzled by what it was, and after looking at it for a moment, he realized one side had a glass "screen," but he tossed it in the back seat. Ronald started his car and let the heater run for a bit during intermission to chase off the damp while he ate. Everything was great, but he wished he had gotten a Coke, too. There was time before the next feature, so Ronald headed back to the concession stand and got a Coke, another chili dog, and some Junior Mints to go with the popcorn. He paid for everything with a crisp new twenty from his wallet and learned from Tom that after *Halloween*, they would be showing *Big Trouble in Little China*.

Ronald walked back to his car and passed a man in a suit, a tie, and a hat, a man who was driving a '52 Ford station wagon. Once back in his car, Ronald settled in, adjusted his speaker, and lost himself. A man in his car surrounded by the sights, smells and the company of the Twilight Drive-In. Ronald felt right at home.

⋏

Eliza Clark had just returned home from her in-laws' with her children. She was exhausted. It had been an emotional night. It was around eleven o'clock, and the children, as wiped out as she was, had kissed her good-night and were off to bed. What a year it had been! So many changes. She wasn't sure she had wanted to attend the service but was glad she had. As emotional as it had been, she felt that her in-laws really needed the support. Eliza walked into the kitchen, sat down at the island, and sighed. Out of the corner of her eye, she could see the old answering machine blinking a "1." She should have gotten rid of that old thing, but Ronald had always been so slow to adapt to new technology, and after everything, she hadn't had the heart to throw it away, even a year later. A year. It seemed like it had been longer. The only real comfort was the insurance. For the first time, she felt financially secure, but guilty as well. He had always tried and, in every other way, had been an exceptional husband and father. She still missed him deeply. He had been the love of her life, but life had not been kind to Ronald. Everything he touched financially had seemed to wither. He was like Sisyphus rolling a stone. Eliza leaned over and hit the play button on the answering machine, leaned back, and listened.

"You have one new message. Message one at 9:15 p.m. 'Hey, sweetie. This is Ronald. I hope you and the kids are okay. I'm on my way, so don't worry. Guess what I just found? A drive-in! Can you believe it? Anyway, I'm going to check it out, maybe get a cup of coffee. I could use a little break. I won't stay long. If it looks good, maybe we can bring the kids sometime. Remember how we used to love it? Okay, then. I'll call you when I get back on the highway. Love you all so much! Bye.'"

Love Story

The kitchen was softly lit by two oil lamps, one on the table and the other on the counter near the wood cookstove. The room was very warm and smelled of strong coffee and frying bacon. A young man, tall with short, dirty-blond hair was adding two eggs to the skillet of bacon sizzling on the stovetop. On the kitchen table, a rifle, ammunition, a Solingen hunting knife, a sharpening stone, and oil were neatly arranged. The man turned his attention to the window over the sink after hearing a dog barking outside. In the half light of early dawn, silhouetted against the snow, he saw a man on horseback approaching the house. The man was wearing a Stetson hat and was bundled up against the bitter cold. The young man watched the rider dismount and then heard him call out to the house, "Paul, it's me, Tom! I'm coming to the door."

Paul pulled the skillet from the heat, wiped his hands on a towel, and walked from the kitchen to the front door and opened it. The air was frigid and had that metallic smell to it that only really cold air has. Paul stepped out onto the porch and, smiling broadly, greeted Tom.

"What the hell are you doing out here in this mess, Tom? Get yourself in here before you freeze solid." Tom stomped the snow off of his boots as he stepped into the warm house. The smell of bacon and coffee was a welcome greeting after the hour-long ride from town in the single-digit cold.

"Coffee?" Paul asked as he stepped back into the kitchen to put the bacon back on.

"Yes, please. Much obliged," Tom replied.

"Have a seat. You care for some breakfast?" Paul asked, still working on the bacon.

"Aw, no thank you. Coffee is fine. Margaret already fed me this morning," said Tom, rubbing his hands together.

Paul poured the coffee for Tom. After pulling the pan off the stovetop, he joined Tom at the table. Tom took a few sips of the coffee, sat the mug down, and cleared his throat. "You're probably wondering what I'm doing up here so early in the morning."

"Someone lost again?" Paul asked, taking a sip of his own coffee.

Tom shook his head gently and looked at the table. "No. No one lost."

"Okay, so what is it? What can I do for you? Everything good?" Paul asked.

Tom took a breath and put his hands on his chin. He looked like he was searching for something.

"I don't know how to say it, Paul, so I'm just gonna say it. I need you to listen to me and let me get all the way through it." Tom held up his right hand as if to pause the moment. Paul, who had a limited circle of people he cared about, struggled to remain quiet and listen. It was as if a ball of lightning were careening around inside of his head. A name and a face washed through his thoughts.

"It's Kimmy. She's passed." Tears were welling up in the old man's eyes, and his voice cracked. "She was found...she...Paul, Kimmy's been killed."

Paul felt a wave of nausea, of anguish, washing over him. What had Tom said? Kimmy's been killed? No, no, no, no, was the response, the mantra in his mind, fighting the horror of what Tom had just put out there. Paul's hands went to his ears as if he could prevent the truth of what Tom had said from penetrating his mind, becoming reality.

Tom sat there for a moment, his mouth slightly agape, a tear running down his right cheek. Tom again held out his right hand as if to stay his younger friend's possible actions. The Winchester was still there on the kitchen table between them, and Tom could see Paul was beginning to shake, to tremble.

"How could this happen, Tom? Was she on the estate?" Paul asked quickly.

"They don't know yet. I wish I had answers for you, but they said they still weren't sure themselves," Tom answered. Tom wanted to get Paul moving. He was worried his young friend would stall with the shock of the news, and he knew it would be better to keep him in motion as much as possible.

"Paul, it's a helluva thing, and I'm so sorry. I truly am. But she needs you now. We should go and get her, take care of her. Can you go with me?" Tom asked, nodding slowly to Paul as if to confirm his own question.

Paul nodded his assent to Tom as tears flowed freely down both cheeks. His hands had come to rest, as if by their own volition, on the rifle lying on the table.

Tom noticed this and placed his right hand on Paul's. "Not now. There may be a time for that, and by God, you know I will be right there with you, but right now let's see to Kimmy."

The two men rode to town in silence beneath slowly falling snow. The road was snowed in and impassible by car. Paul felt himself drifting as if in a dream, images of his wife filling his mind, interrupted only by the anguish-inducing knowledge that he would never see, hold, or kiss her again. Paul had had his misgivings about Kimmy working on the estate, and he felt guilt creeping into him. It had been part of the plan, he reminded himself, part of the plan to buy Tom out and take over the guide business. Paul had hated being away from Kimmy, but the money she was earning on the estate was very good and would expedite the two of them becoming financially independent. Kimmy also confessed to Paul that she enjoyed the work and confessed to herself that she'd found a certain romance in the title of "governess." To Kimmy, the position, which was something of a rarity in the United States, made her feel as though she were a character in a Victorian novel. Paul had never heard Kimmy express any misgivings about her employer other than to say that he was "an eccentric." Paul wondered if his pride was to blame. Tom had offered to sign the business holdings over to him and allow him to pay them off over time, but Paul would have none of that, preferring that Tom be paid in full before he and Kimmy took over. Once they had paid Tom, the plan had been for Paul to run the guide service and operate the cabins, while Kimmy would take a job as a teacher at the local school. It would have been a perfect life. Would have been. In Paul's mind, a hundred variables came and went. So many things could have changed the course of events, the outcome. If one of these had been different, Kimmy would surely still be alive.

They were met at the train station by Tom's wife, Margaret. Margaret and Tom had been like a mother and father to Paul, and he found himself unable to hold back his grief in Margaret's presence. Tom discreetly left the two alone for a bit, allowing his wife to console his young friend. Tom felt inadequate for the task.

They learned via telegraph that Kimberly's body would arrive the next morning. Paul took Tom and Margaret up on their invitation to stay with them in town that night. Paul neither ate nor slept. Questions swirled through his mind as to how the woman he loved could be murdered on the lavish private estate where she was employed as a governess. Tom had confirmed through his contacts in New York that Kimberly had been found on the grounds at dawn the previous day by workers moving firewood to the main house. Kimberly stayed in a cottage near the main house at night, and police told Tom there had been no sign of a break-in or disturbance at the cottage.

Tom's previous life as a Pinkerton meant he had friends in law enforcement throughout the east, but especially New York, both city and state. Through a series of telegraphs, Tom had learned that the owner of the estate, a Mr. Thomas Boncras, had an interesting and alarmingly notable reputation. Since his teens, Mr. Boncras had been involved in numerous scandals involving young women, some of them in the employ of his family. While never arrested for any crime, it was pretty well known in the right circles that Thomas Boncras was, at best, an indelicate woman-izer and, at worst, a rapist and assaulter of women. Being wealthy and well connected, Mr. Boncras's family had managed to protect him from justice and the responsibility of this various transgres-sions. With this in mind, Paul sat fitfully in the dark that night, his own nature and the loss of his wife putting him in a state of mind that grieved and called for revenge at the same time.

Tom and Margaret had been like a mother and father to him, taking him in and giving him a chance when no one else would. Paul had started doing odd jobs around their small farm and hunting cabins when he was just a skinny sixteen-year-old. As the second of six children raised on a coal miner's wages, Paul's childhood had been hard. His mother and two of his siblings had died of consumption, and his father had died in a mine accident when Paul was only fourteen. Paul's remaining siblings had gone to live with various relatives, but Paul had decided to go east instead of into the mines. The young man had eventually found his way to the northeast corner of Pennsylvania. Paul had been hunting since he was a young boy, and the idea of being able to be in the woods appealed to him greatly. Tom and Margaret had taken an immediate liking to the lanky, towheaded young man whom they found to be hardworking and honest. As Paul grew into manhood, he grew closer and closer to the couple and they to him. People in town began to refer to Paul as "that Thompson boy," assuming he was their son, adopted or otherwise. It was a title Paul had been proud to assume.

Margaret was the picture of kindness, love, and charity and Tom a steady, wise teacher—a fine example for Paul to follow.

Paul had learned from others around town that Tom had been at San Juan Hill with Roosevelt and had nearly died of his wounds, something that Tom had never shared with him personally, and Paul had deemed it wise not to ask him about it. After the war, Tom had taken a job with the Pinkertons, a fact that had initially given Paul mixed feelings, being that the coal miners in his family had often been at odds with the organization. After much thought, Paul had decided that a man as good as Tom was one of "the good" Pinkertons. After all, his mother had taught him there was good in everyone if you looked hard enough. The hardest thing for Paul to square about Tom was the stories of how rough he had been in his previous profession. People who had known Tom their whole lives told stories about his prowess with a gun and the numerous shootings he had been involved in while a Pinkerton. Paul never heard Tom speak of his past life, and the man gave him no reason to question his goodness, so Paul decided long ago to leave it at that.

Tom and Paul rose early, but Margaret even earlier, preparing breakfast for the two men. After eating in relative silence, Tom and Paul bundled up, hitched up the wagon, and headed to the rail station. There were few cars and trucks moving because of the snow, and the streets had an eerie, lonely quality to them. For Paul, the whole thing was surreal, as if he were in someone else's body. Kimmy couldn't really be dead; she was too alive. Paul had never met anyone so alive, so full of life. As the two men stood in the pale morning light waiting on the platform, the station manager, knowing what Paul and Tom had come for, asked the men to come in out of the cold.

"May as well wait inside with me," he said. "Got coffee on." He shook his head mournfully and added, "Such a loss, such a loss."

Paul turned away from the well-meaning man so he couldn't see the tears in his eyes and answered, "Kind of you, sir, but if my Kimmy's out in this, it's the least I can do to be out in it, too."

The station manager, having no words, nodded solemnly, turned, and walked back into the station.

Tom and Paul waited in silence, Tom lighting his pipe and Paul simply staring into space as if in the void he might find a way out of this nightmare. Paul thought about meeting Kimberly for the first time. "Kimberly" is what she had called herself and what her well-to-do family from Albany had called her. Paul had been employed by her father as a hunting guide, and the man's family had accompanied him to one of the big cabins that Tom had maintained in the mountains west of town. Tom had gotten into the business soon after meeting Margaret and over the years had turned it into a profitable business. Paul had been a natural. He had been hunting since he was old enough to pick up a rifle or shotgun and was adept at skinning and processing game of all kinds. More than that, Paul had a good way about him. For a young man, he was well spoken and tended to command the deference of his often-older clients. Kimberly and Paul had fallen for each other almost immediately, much to the chagrin of her father, who, although he respected Paul as a hunting guide, thought him beneath his daughter's station. When it became clear that the two would not be parted, her father had demanded that Tom fire Paul and put an end to the relationship. It was the only time Paul had seen a glimpse of the "old Tom" he had heard so many stories about. The look in Tom's eyes had probably been enough to wither Kimmy's father, Mr. Vandevander, but for good measure, Tom had informed him coolly that no man dictated what he would or would not do, and that any more slights cast against his son, Paul, would be taken as a personal insult and dealt with accordingly.

Mr. Vandevander had chosen to back down from Tom but had then shunned his daughter. Tom and Margaret had insisted that Paul stay at one of the smaller cabins while Kimberly settled into the house in town with them. The separation hadn't lasted long, as the two were married soon after and installed themselves into the small-but-cozy cabin a few miles from town. It had been the most amazing time of his life. The two fished and hiked the mountains, and Kimberly painted landscapes and read to Paul. Paul taught Kimberly to shoot and was impressed that she insisted on learning how to process game, and Kimberly was impressed that the man she loved was humble enough to ask her to teach him to read. The two had been a perfect complement to each other.

The train arrived punctually at 8:00 a.m. The conductor, who was an old friend of Tom's, came to the platform to supervise the unloading of Kimberly's remains personally. The large, bearded man removed his hat, put his hand on Paul's shoulder, and said simply, "If I may be of further service to you, sir, you have but to ask."

Paul nodded, trying not to look the man in the eye out of an unconscious fear that he might see into his pain, his weakness. Once the wooden box containing Kimberly had been loaded into the wagon, Tom and Paul took her across town to Parr and Sons. Old Man Parr had been the town's undertaker for as long as anyone could remember, and his father before him. As they pulled around to the back of the large brick establishment, they found Mr. Parr and his two sons dressed immaculately, waiting for them like an honor guard.

"Mr. Thompson," Mr. Parr said, extending his hand to Paul. "Please accept my condolences for your grievous loss. My family and I would be honored if you would allow us to care for your beloved from here." With that he had bowed deeply, his sons mirroring their father. Standing upright, he then added, "One of my sons will bring word when we have made ready for you."

"Thank you, Mr. Parr," Paul managed, knowing it was a polite way of saying they needed a night to thaw Kimberly's body, as it must be frozen solid from a day in a freight car. Mr. Parr nodded and snapped his fingers, and his two sons deftly transferred the box to a four-wheeled cart and moved her down a ramp and through a set of double doors into the basement of the building.

Paul felt sick the whole ride home. Upon arriving at Tom and Margaret's, Paul asked their leave and retired to his room upstairs where he finally broke down and wept. At some point, he fell asleep, the deep sleep of the those exhausted by the torment of loss. The kind of sleep that is more an escape than rest. Paul was awakened by Tom and surprised to hear it was around ten in the morning. How had he slept so long?

"Mr. Parr's boy was here, Paul. They're ready for you now," Tom said, looking him in the eye.

"Margaret's got some coffee and sandwiches for you, Paul. You should eat something before you go."

Paul looked down and shook his head. "Please tell her thanks, but I should go. Tell her I'll eat when I get back. I should..." There was a pause.

Tom put his hand on Paul's shoulder and spoke softly. "I know, Paul. She knows. Maybe I should go with you."

Paul shook his head, still looking at the floor. "Thank you, but I need to do this myself. Better go."

"All right, then. All right," said Tom, stepping aside.

Paul dressed hurriedly and left the house. The snow had stopped falling, and it seemed colder than before. The sky was a somber leaden color, and it was very still. Paul looked at the ground and hardly noticed the people he passed on the street. If he had, he would have seen the men remove their hats and the women put their gloved hands to their faces as he passed. Everyone in the small town had heard the news of Kimberly's death. She and Paul had both been well liked in a town that didn't normally take to outsiders.

The walk took about ten minutes, and at times Paul felt as if he were drunk, like he was floating the distance to Parr's. The entrance to Parr and Sons was a grand set of double doors, heavily molded and flanked by two tall Greek columns. Paul lifted the large brass knocker and gave two raps on the door, and after a moment, Mr. Parr himself opened it and motioned for Paul to enter with a sweep of his left arm and a slight bow.

"Please, Mr. Thompson. Please come in from the cold," he said, closing the doors as Paul stepped inside.

One of Mr. Parr's sons (they both looked the same) took Paul's coat and hat and hung them from a brass coatrack to the right of the door. The entry was floored in white marble that terminated at the interior, giving way to a well-polished hardwood floor covered here and there with tasteful oriental rugs. The walls were wainscoted, with pleasant blue floral wallpaper covering the top half. In this main hall, there were several couches and chairs as well as tables placed strategically throughout to accommodate the grieving, and the room was lit from above by an ornate crystal chandelier as well as wall sconces.

Mr. Parr positioned himself in front of Paul, dressed in his typical immaculate black suit, his posture erect and dignified. The man's sons stood to the left, demonstrating an equal posture. The older man had dark hair graying at the temples and a prominent mustache.

Mr. Parr gently cleared his throat and spoke. "Mr. Thompson, again please accept our most sincere condolences for your loss. Your beloved is in repose below." He paused for a moment and his head tilted slightly downward. "We have done what was possible in the time we were given, but I must inform you that with more time, she could be made more presentable to you before you see her if you wish it so."

Paul looked from Mr. Parr to his sons and back again before he spoke. None of them betrayed any emotion.

"I would very much like to see her now, sir," Paul managed.

Mr. Parr gave a short nod in assent. "Of course, Mr. Thompson. I assumed that would be so. If you will follow me."

With that, Mr. Parr turned on his right heel and, motioning for Paul to follow, walked through an archway into a long, carpeted hallway lit by wall sconces and stopped at a door about halfway down the hall. Mr. Parr unlocked the door with a key he produced from his jacket, pushed it open, and started down a set of stairs. Paul, close behind, started down the stairs behind Mr. Parr.

"Please mind your step, Mr. Thompson," Mr. Parr said over his shoulder as he continued downward.

At the bottom of the stairs, there was a landing and an oak door with a frosted-glass window. Mr. Parr opened the door and stepped into a large, well-lit room. The floor was covered in white tile, and the walls were covered to the ceiling with smaller white tiles. Lighting was provided by wall fixtures as well as fixtures suspended from the ceiling. There were three enameled-steel tables spaced evenly across the center of the room and glass-doored cabinets along the right wall containing all the myriad tools and chemicals needed for Mr. Parr's trade. Only the center table was occupied, the figure lying on it covered with a white cloth. Paul, seeing this as he entered the space, faltered, and an audible, heavy sigh escaped his lips. Mr. Parr turned and gently took Paul's right arm and shoulder, steadying him.

"Do you wish to continue, Mr. Thompson?" Mr. Parr asked quietly. "Perhaps you need to retire upstairs for a bit to collect yourself?"

Paul took a deep breath, straightened himself, and shook his head. "No…no. I am fine. I need to do this. Thank you."

Mr. Parr nodded and released Paul from his gentle grip. Moving to the center table, he lifted the sheet and carefully folded it down, revealing Kimberly. A second sheet had been placed over the body up to her collarbones and tucked under her armpits, allowing only her head, neck, and arms to remain exposed. Mr. Parr, upon completing this task, moved to the left wall away from Kimberly. Folding his hands in front of him, he said, "Please take whatever time you require. Would you like me to step out?"

Paul shook his head and stepped forward around the first table, and as he stood next to Kimberly, he felt himself falter once more. Mr. Parr took a step forward, his arms extended as if to catch the man should he collapse. Paul raised his left arm and waved the man back. Mr. Parr returned to the wall and resumed his former pose.

As Paul regarded his wife's body, he was struck and sickened by the violence evident. Kimberly's face bore the bruises and cuts of a beating. Both eyes were swollen shut, her lips torn. Kimberly's forearms exhibited heavy bruising as well. Paul gently placed his right hand on his wife's head, feeling the softness of her blond hair. Unconsciously, his left hand found hers, and he held it gently. How cold it was, this hand that once touched his face, this small, beautiful hand. Paul lifted her hand to his face and kissed it, and as he did, tears began to flow from his eyes.

"I'm so sorry, my love," he muttered. "Oh, Kimmy, what did he do to you?"

Still clasping her hand, he leaned in close to her face and gently kissed her cheek. "Oh, God! Oh, God, Kimmy, I love you so…" he whispered to her, his tears falling upon her face.

At that moment, the bulbs in the wall fixtures and the overhead lights exploded, plunging the room into darkness.

Paul thought he felt Kimberly's left hand squeeze his and heard her voice as clear as glass say, "Avenge me, Paul! Avenge me!"

Mr. Parr had fled the room, finding the exit and bolting from the basement in a state of panic. Mr. Parr's sons, going to their father and being unable to discern the cause of his distress, had gone into the basement. Finding the lights inoperable, they had retrieved lanterns and, going back down, discovered Paul unconscious on the floor at the base of his wife's table.

Mr. Parr never spoke of what he experienced that day in the basement and would take no further part in the preparation of Kimberly's body, instead delegating this task to his sons. Paul likewise kept the events to himself. Tom and Margaret took no real note of his silence. After all, how else would one be expected to behave after such tragedy? The funeral was a muted, somber affair as all funerals are, particularly winter funerals, and although many from town attended, Paul felt he was the only one there, alone in his grief. Kimberly's parents had declined to attend, such being the depth of their estrangement from their daughter. It was generally agreed in their family that this sort of thing was a logical result of consorting with those beneath them.

⋏

In the time following Kimberly's funeral, Paul had been at the mercy of several masters. In the fore was his grief and not far behind that was anger, a need to exact justice for Kimberly. Lurking behind it all, Paul thought about that moment in the basement of Parr's. He was sure it had not been imagined. The lights had exploded; he had felt her grip, heard her voice. Was it true? Had she spoken? He had heard it. He was sure Mr. Parr had heard it as well. More than simply hearing it, Paul had felt it. A plea for reckoning he carried in his heart and mind, a thing deeply and reverently borne.

As the winter days dragged on, the quest for that reckoning seemed no closer. Tom had been able to ferret out a great deal about the case from his various police contacts, and it seemed, at least off the record, that the general consensus among those who had worked the case was that the murder had been committed by someone on the estate. In the first place, the estate was fairly secluded, far from the nearest town. In the second, there were too many servants, many of them working during the time the murder was thought to have occurred, to make it plausible that some stranger had wandered onto the grounds and committed the deed undetected. The police had interviewed all of the staff and found it remarkable that not one of them had anything of value to share. Mr. Boncras had not been interviewed until nearly two weeks after the crime, and only then under protest from his lawyers. In confidence, Tom had learned from his contacts still active in law enforcement that the higher-ups had made it clear that detectives were to desist from pursuing Mr. Boncras and focus on finding the "intruder" who must be responsible for this heinous act. Also shared with Tom—in confidence, of course—was the belief by those closest to the investigation that the perpetrator must be Mr. Boncras. They believed that only he had the history, even if it was off the books, to indicate he could have committed such an act. They also believed that because he operated the estate like a lord, none of the estate's staff would ever bring testimony against him.

As time wore on, Paul's anger grew. The idea that he should take things into his own hands began to grow stronger and stronger, as did his deep state of melancholy. Paul stayed on with Tom and Margaret for several weeks after the funeral, hoping that Tom's digging might bear fruit, but any hope he had of legal justice disappeared one evening. Tom returned home from the telegraph office and called Paul into the kitchen, saying he had news of the case. Paul felt immediate anxiety because of Tom's demeanor. It reminded him of the morning Tom had delivered the news of Kimberly's death to him at the cabin, but he tried to hold out hope. Tom sat at the head of the kitchen table, and Paul pulled up a chair to his right. Margaret asked the two if they would like coffee, but both men politely declined, so she took her leave. Tom was absentmindedly stroking his moustache with his left index finger while he gazed past Paul at the big wooden cookstove as if it somehow held the words he must say. Paul leaned toward the older man, putting a hand on his shoulder.

"Look at me, Tom," Paul said evenly. "Tell me. What news?"

Without moving his head, Tom directed his gaze at Paul, looking him directly in the eyes. After a moment, Tom spoke. "The boys up in New York arrested a fella for Kimmy's murder, Paul," he said. Paul removed his hand from Tom's shoulder and leaned back in his chair, exhaling deeply as he did.

"Boncras, right? They arrested him?" Paul said.

Tom shook his head slowly.

"Then who? Someone else did this?" Paul asked, leaning forward, his arms crossed on the table.

Tom followed suit, folding his arms on the table in front of him before he answered. "The people whom I believe say it was not someone else who did it, but all the same, someone else has been arrested for it."

Paul looked down at his hands and then up at Tom. Tom put his left hand up to his temple before he continued. "The higher-ups needed to close this. They couldn't touch Boncras," Tom began before Paul interrupted him.

"Why not, goddamn it?" Paul exploded. "If everyone knows he did this, he killed Kimmy, why not? He's a murderer and worse, and he'll just walk?" Paul said, banging his right fist on the table-top. Tom remained as he was, not reacting to his friend's anger.

"Paul," Tom replied, "It's worse than that, even."

Paul clenched his fists and leaned toward Tom, his eyes angry slits. "How? Worse how?" he hissed.

Tom folded his hands on the table in front of him and leaned back a bit.

"The law up there made a sweep through a hobo camp a few miles from the estate," Tom said. "They rounded up some fellows, transients living near the train tracks up there."

Paul nodded.

Tom cleared his throat and continued. "They worked these fellas over till they got some of 'em to make statements against one of the others. After that, they leaned on this man, a feeble-minded sort, until they got a full confession from him. They got it all wrapped up. Nice and neat."

The men sat in silence for a few moments, the only sound that of the fire crackling in the stove. Paul put his face in his hands and rocked slowly back and forth. Tom broke the silence and spoke. "They have their conviction. They will hang this man, Paul. There's nothing to be done about—"

"Nothing!" Paul exclaimed, dropping his hands and shouting. "Nothing? I'll tell you what I'm doing, Tom. I'm going to go up there and kill that bastard! That's what I'm doing! 'Nothing,' you say to me? To *me*?"

Tom straightened up in his chair, a look of rage in his eyes. "Damn it, Paul!" Tom erupted, taking Paul by surprise. "Listen to me when I say it gets worse! An innocent man is going to die for what happened to Kimmy, and Boncras..." Tom paused. "Boncras is gone. Gone to Europe somewhere. Too much pressure this time, too much. Apparently, all of this shitbird's favors are used up. He's been exiled, out of reach. Look at me, Paul, and listen." Tom put his hand on his friend's shoulder. Paul looked him in the eye. "You know if I thought we could get this bastard, I'd be talking about some kind of plan. I'd be with you all the way. You know that, don't you?"

Paul nodded in assent. Tom nodded as well, and then continued. "I don't know when or if he'll be back here. No way to tell. People like Boncras have deep pockets and deeper connections. Even if we could find him, I don't see how we could get to him. I've done a lot of man tracking in my day, brought a lot of bad people in, put a lot of bad men down, but this is beyond me. It's beyond us, Paul."

A tear was running down Paul's cheek. Tom, choked up, cleared his throat. "I'm sorry," he said, squeezing Paul's shoulder.

Paul left for the cabin the next morning despite Tom and Margaret's pleas that he stay with them a while longer. Margaret confided in Tom that she worried how Paul would fare in the cabin alone. Margaret worried that, surrounded by so much to remind him of his lost love, his grief would overwhelm him. Tom tried to quiet her fears, saying he had seen other men lose as much, even more, and go on with their lives. The truth was that Tom was trying to convince himself as much as he was trying to convince his wife that all would be well.

Each day seemed to Paul an eternity; the house, which had once been the site of so much love, warmth, and hope, was reduced to a prison of sadness and desperation. The days since learning of Kimberly's murder began to fuse together. Paul ate and slept little, and his body mirrored the anguish that plagued his mind. As January gave way to February, Paul had become virtually a hermit, sitting for hours a day, lost in his deepening sadness. Paul slept only when the exhaustion of his emotional state forced it upon him, and while he slept, he was haunted by dreams. In his dreams, he would see the incident in Parr's basement, sometimes Kimmy standing before him, speaking to him but making no sound. When he would awaken, he would find himself disoriented and alone in the cold, dark cabin.

Paul did the bare minimum of self-care, keeping the fire only enough to prevent freezing to death, and eating mostly cold leftovers of what Margaret and Tom would bring him every few days. By the middle of February, Tom and Margaret, shocked by his appearance and the way he was existing, begged him to come back to town with them, but Paul had refused.

"I think we need to get him out of there, Margaret," Tom told his wife after their last visit to the cabin. "I'm worried for him now, but I don't think he'll come willingly."

Margaret nodded. "Maybe we should get some help for him." Margaret answered.

"Melancholia's what they call it," Tom said. "Saw some men after the war, good men, fall into it."

"What happened to them?" Margaret asked, looking afraid.

Tom paused before answering his wife, measuring his answer. "Well, hon, it can get bad. Depends on the man."

"You don't think Paul could do something to hurt himself, do you? You don't think he would..." Margaret said, choking up.

Tom patted his wife's hand affectionately and leaned in close to her. "No, no, Margaret. I'll not let it come to that, dear. I think I'll go see Doc Turner. We'll go out tomorrow and see Paul, see to it that he's okay. How would that be, love?"

"Yes. Please do that. I worry so about that poor boy," Margaret said, tears flowing from her eyes.

Tom paid Dr. Turner a visit that afternoon, and after explaining the situation to him, the doctor agreed they should go out the next morning.

"Paul is armed, I assume?" The doctor asked Tom.

"Of course he is, Doc," Tom answered. "He works in the woods, hunting, guiding, you know. He's got a Winchester, a couple of shotguns, the Colt I gave him."

Dr. Turner suggested they bring a deputy with them, just in case. Tom, while insisting Paul would be no danger to them, finally agreed to the doctor's terms. The plan would be to let Dr. Turner talk to Paul and evaluate whether or not he should be brought in for his own protection.

"If we have to bring him in," Tom asked, "where would he be placed? Not in jail."

"Of course not. Maybe the sanatorium for a bit, just till we can get him back to his old self."

"He's not crazy!" Tom protested. "He just lost his wife. He's in a state of grief!"

Dr. Turner held his hands up in front of him. "I know he's not crazy. I didn't mean to imply any such thing. But if he's as low as you say he is, it may be the only thing that keeps him alive. Where else would he stay? If we can get him from the cabin, where else would he stay willingly? Our options are limited, Tom. You of all people should know that. I want to help, and the whole town grieved his loss, including me, so know that I don't take this lightly."

Tom nodded and put his hand to his brow. "Of course, Doc. I know. You're a good man, and that's why I came to you. But the sanatorium? I wish there were some other way."

"So do I. That's the final option. Let's go out there tomorrow, see how he's doing, and go from there," the doctor said.

That evening, as Dr. Turner and Tom conspired on Paul's behalf, Paul slipped the final distance from grief and sadness into despair. That evening, as the long winter night began, Paul reached an epiphany. He was tired, and as he walked through the cabin that had been his and Kimmy's home, he saw only disorder, heard only silence. Each room was in disarray, as if reflecting the ruined state of his life. Paul lit an oil lamp, picked it up, and made his way to the bathroom. Placing the lamp on the washstand, he regarded himself in the mirror. Was this him? Was this haggard, wasted figure even him? To Paul, it was as if he were trapped in this shell, the shell of a dying man, a man dying from the inside out. As he peered into the eyes of the bearded figure in the mirror, Paul muttered to himself. "I can't, Kimmy. I'm sorry. I'm so tired. I wanted to get him, but I just need to be with you now."

Paul reached over and picked up his razor with his right hand. He opened it, exposing the blade. He placed his left hand on the edge of the washstand, gripping it tightly, bracing himself. Paul's right hand, grasping the razor tightly, brought it up to the left side of his throat. He could feel the cold edge of the razor resting on the skin of his throat, the bite of that edge already cutting into him. He braced himself again, closing his eyes in preparation of the act, the act that would release him from this torment. In this moment, a drop of Paul's blood ran down the edge of the razor and fell into the basin below. The effect was instantaneous. Even with his eyes closed, Paul felt something happening. The temperature of the room fell suddenly, the chill moving through his body. He heard a crackling sound like ice on a river fracturing. Paul heard a voice, not a voice in his head, but a loud, clear voice. Paul would know that voice anywhere. It was Kimmy saying one word: "No!"

Paul opened his eyes, his body frozen. The mirror in front of him was frosted over by the cold, the glass spiderwebbed with hundreds of cracks. Still frozen in place, Paul's eyes darted to the left and right, searching. As he exhaled, he could see his breath. Besides the cold, Paul felt something else, a presence in the room with him. In a weak, shaky tone, he muttered out loud, "Kimmy?"

"Put it down, Paul," he heard Kimmy say. "Put down the razor. You're not done. I'm with you, love."

Paul slowly opened his right hand, and the razor fell with a clatter into the basin. The room immediately became warmer. He became warmer, too, as if he were slipping into a bath. Paul released his grip on the washstand and took a step back. "Kimmy, is it really you?" he asked, wondering if he could trust his own ears.

"It is me, Paul. This is real. You're not crazy. You weren't crazy at Parr's either. I was there, too. Do you remember what I asked you to do?" Kimmy said.

"Avenge you," Paul said. "You asked me to avenge you, Kimmy, and I wanted to. I, I tried, but the police let him go. He's gone."

"I know, Paul. I know you tried. I know you wanted to get justice. I know he's gone away, but we'll bring him back. We have help."

"I'm sorry, Kimmy," Paul said, sobbing. "I'm sorry for what happened to you, sorry I wasn't there."

"I know, and I'm sorry for what you've been through, how you've suffered, but it will be okay. We'll never be apart again. We have a task to finish here, Paul, justice to be meted out. I wasn't the first woman he hurt. We will stop him," Kimmy said.

Paul nodded and wiped his face. A sense of calm had washed over him. Kimmy was here. Paul knew it was real because for the first time since the news of Kimmy's death, he didn't feel alone. "What do we have to do, Kimmy?" Paul asked, feeling his old self returning.

"Tom is coming tomorrow. He and Margaret are so worried about you. They love you so much. Tom is bringing some people here tomorrow to look in on you and see if you're in danger."

There was a pause. Paul nodded, closing his eyes, and Kimmy continued. "You have to convince them you are well, my love, that you aren't in danger. Put yourself, our home, in order, Paul."

In the hours that followed, Paul set about the task of putting the cabin and himself in order. Paul got the fires going in the kitchen stove and the fireplace, heated water, bathed, shaved, and changed his clothes. He then went from room to room, picking up, dusting, sweeping, and mopping. Paul felt a ravenous hunger, and when he had finished with the cabin, he cooked dinner for himself, the first real one he had eaten since Kimmy's death, consisting of venison stew and biscuits with black coffee to wash it all down. Between the food and the feeling of relief he felt from Kimmy's return, Paul felt a kind of sleepiness brought on by deep contentment, so after dinner, he crawled into bed and fell asleep while conversing with his wife.

The next morning, Tom rose early, before dawn. Sitting up in bed, he took in the quiet. A sudden feeling of panic washed over him. Had it all been a dream? Had he imagined her back?

"Kimmy? Are you here?" Paul called out to the empty room.

"I'm here, Paul. I told you we wouldn't be apart again."

Relieved, Paul dressed, tended the fires, shoveled the snow from the porch, and returning to the kitchen, he began to prepare breakfast. As Paul performed these menial, everyday tasks, he wondered if he had lost his mind. The only other possibility was that Kimmy's spirit was with him. Paul was a believer; he believed in God, in spirits, but to hear them? To hear her? In the end, whether this was real or a product of his grief-stricken mind, he would follow her. The only other choice was the way of loneliness and desperation.

As Paul sat down to eat his breakfast, he heard a vehicle pull up to the gate. The doors closed, and then he heard a familiar voice call out from the yard, "Paul? It's Tom."

Paul rose from the table, walked to the front door, opened it, and stepped out onto the porch. Tom approached the cabin, accompanied by three other men. Paul recognized them immediately. The large, rotund man to his left was Dr. Turner, and the other two following close behind were Sheriff Williams and Deputy Cooper. The two lawmen appeared edgy as they trod through the snow onto the path he had shoveled. Both men were wearing guns under their coats, which were unbuttoned. It appeared they had come prepared for trouble. Tom was smiling broadly, and as he came up to the porch steps, Paul could see a look of puzzlement behind the smile as though Tom were seeing something he did not expect.

"Morning, Tom," Paul said evenly. "If I'd known I was having company, I would have made you fellas breakfast. I was just sitting down to it myself."

Tom studied Paul for a moment. Although he still looked gaunt, Paul was clean-shaven and dressed in clean clothes. There was something else about Paul, something different in his demeanor that was hard for Tom to qualify. Making a sweep toward his companions with his left arm, Tom spoke. "Good morning to you. I hope this isn't an intrusion. You know these fellas already, so I guess there's no need to introduce everybody. We just came out here this morning to look in on you, see if you were doing all right."

Paul nodded and smiled, acknowledging each of the men. "That's really thoughtful of you all. Come on in out of the cold. I've got coffee. I'm sure you could all use a cup. Long ride out here." Paul motioned them in, holding the door for them as they trundled into the cabin, stomping the snow from their boots and hanging their coats. After all were seated in the kitchen and coffee had been poured, there was an awkward silence, the men glancing at Paul and then at each other. The silence was broken when Dr. Turner cleared his throat and spoke.

"I'd like to apologize again for coming unannounced. I suppose it seems strange to you that Tom brought us out," Dr. Turner said, looking at Paul carefully. "The truth is that Tom and Margaret have been worried about you. You've been through a lot these past weeks. How are you holding up, Paul?"

Paul looked at the men seated at his table. Tom looked particularly uncomfortable with the situation, so he reached out with his right hand and gently clutched Tom's shoulder. "I appreciate your concern," he said, looking Tom in the eyes. "I know I've worried you to death, and I'm sorry. Please tell Margaret that, too. I'm lucky to have you both. I can't thank you two enough for all you've done for me."

Tom nodded slowly and replied. "No need to apologize. You're a son to us. I didn't mean to overstep."

Paul took his hand from Tom's shoulder and waved it dismissively as he shook his head, looking down at his coffee. "You're the one who doesn't need to apologize, Tom. I know I've not been myself. I must have seemed crazy these past weeks. I understand what you're doing, and I hope I would do the same if you were in my place. So thank you."

"I understand, you know," Dr. Turner interjected. The other four men turned their attention to the doctor as he continued. "I lost my wife Catherine some years ago, and it's no secret that I went through a rough patch afterward. For me, it was whiskey. It took me years and the help of the almighty," the Doctor said, gesturing toward the heavens, "to find my way past my grief. A man can become hopeless, adrift." Dr. Turner took a sip of his coffee and glanced around the room. "It appears you are managing in spite of your loss."

"Trying to," Paul replied. "I know I'm not done, but I'm trying to get back."

The elephant in the room exposed, the remainder of the visit passed with Paul's visitors offering their condolences and support. To Tom, the transformation Paul had undergone was nothing short of a miracle, the only sign of harm to Paul being a small cut under his left jaw, probably from shaving. As the men departed, Paul watched them from the porch. A light snow fell as the car started and drove away.

"Tom looked relieved," Kimmy said. She had remained silent during the visit, and Paul was glad to hear her voice again.

"He did. They've been through a lot, too. They loved you so," Paul said, watching the snow fall.

Paul went inside, tidied up the kitchen, and poured himself another cup of coffee. As he sat at the table, he felt at odds. One side of him felt content, the other side filled with questions. "Kimmy, could I ask you something? Not about the end, but about after that. What happened? What comes next?"

"I don't understand it all," Kimmy answered. "I was able to look down to see myself. I had no fear. I felt so warm and safe. Then it was like being pulled, like being drawn away."

"Away from life?" Paul asked.

"No. Not from life. I don't know how to describe it. Away from pain and doubt and fear. I don't think this is life. I think this is only a part of life."

"How? How did you come back to me?"

"God," Kimmy said. "I think it was God. Had to be. He spoke to me. God told me what I had to do, to come to you."

"Did you see God, Kimmy?" Paul asked.

"No. I didn't see Him. I felt Him, all around me, through me. I don't think I was meant to see God yet." Kimmy's voice sounded sad.

"When, then? When can you see God?"

"There was an opening, a gate, a window maybe. It was light, soft, and warm, and I knew that goodness filled the other side of it. Heaven is what I thought. Heaven is on the other side. God was in front of it like a keeper. God told me that after I had finished the task given to me, I could come home."

"Justice," Paul whispered.

"Exactly," Kimmy answered.

That day, Kimmy explained what needed to happen next, what they needed to do. The next morning, Paul was to hike up to the pond. The pond was located about halfway up the mountain behind the cabin, located at the site of an abandoned farm, its owners long dead. The only visible remnants of the farm were the home's fireplace and the pond. The pond was small, maybe a quarter of an acre, and at its north edge was a huge, ancient willow. Paul knew this place well. Kimmy and Paul had spent many summer evenings here. Under the shade of the big willow, Kimmy would read to Paul, the works of Homer, Cooper, and others on Kimmy's lips as they lay on a blanket.

Paul rose early, ate a quick breakfast, dressed, and began the trek up the mountain. As he walked, Paul's mind was flooded with memories. How many times had he walked this trail with

Kimmy? As he hiked, he and Kimmy reminisced about their time on the mountain—some of their dearest memories. Reaching the brushy field where the pond was located, Paul took it all in. The sky was clear and pale blue, the air was cold, and hoarfrost covered the grass and brush around the pond. The drooping branches of the willow covered in frost twinkled and shimmered in the morning sun, giving it a magical quality. Paul walked to the base of the willow. The pond was frozen over and was covered with a pristine layer of snow. It was so still, no wind blew. Paul only felt the cold around him.

"What now, Kimmy?" Paul asked, taking in the scene.

"The chimney, Paul," Kimmy answered. "Look at the chimney."

Paul turned to his left, away from the willow and the pond. The fireplace was about twenty feet high, constructed of limestone. It looked like some out-of-place monolith in this wilderness. Some of the mortar had crumbled away in spots, particularly near the top, and the stones above were covered in several inches of fresh snow.

"What am I looking for, Kimmy?" Paul asked, looking over the fireplace.

"Wait, Paul. Look."

He continued to look at the fireplace. There was nothing to hint at what he was looking for. "Kimmy—" Paul began.

"Paul, look!"

From about a hundred yards behind the fireplace, Paul saw movement. A bird, a large bird, had broken from the tree line and was flying toward them. From the look of the bird, it was some kind of raptor. It landed on the top of the fireplace, the snow exploding around it, creating a dramatic effect. Being only fifty feet or so from the fireplace, Paul could clearly make out the details of the bird's appearance. Perhaps most prominent were the bird's eyes, bright and piercing, the color of marigolds in bloom.

"Goshawk! It's a goshawk!" Paul exclaimed with wonder.

Paul had spent much of his life in the wilds hunting and fishing. While no expert on birds, he had seen many goshawks in his time afield, but he had never had the opportunity to regard one in such close proximity. Many outdoorsmen shot birds of prey on sight—redtails, coopers, and also goshawks. The typical wisdom was that these birds, if left alone, would "kill out all of the game." Paul, however, had never shared this view. It seemed improbable to him that these birds were a detriment to small game populations. If such views were true, how was it that the early settlers reported such an abundance of game? Beyond his logical views about hawks, Paul had always admired these birds and their power. They were hunters like himself. He felt a kinship with them and could never bring himself to kill one. Paul stared at the goshawk for several minutes, expecting the bird to fly at any moment.

"She's here to help, Paul," Kimmy said.

"How could she help?"

"So many questions!" Kimmy said, giggling. "Have a little faith, love."

"Okay," Paul said. "Now what?"

"Hold up your arm."

Without a word, Paul held up his right arm. There was a brief pause. The goshawk leaned slightly forward and, with a few beats of her great wings, was airborne. It only took a moment for the bird to reach Paul and alight onto his forearm. First of all, the landing had been much gentler than he had expected. Second, even through the sleeve of his wool coat, Paul could feel the goshawk's talons, sharp as needles, digging into his arm. Paul's pain was forgotten by the proximity of the bird; he was face-to-face with the goshawk. The bird was about two feet high and was a dark-slate color except for its breast, which was white with black barring.

"She likes you," Kimmy said. "She knows a hunter when she sees one. Let's go home, Paul."

"What about her?" Paul asked, unsure what to do about the bird on his arm.

"She'll follow us. Let's go."

Paul turned and began to walk out of the clearing, and the goshawk gently lifted off and glided to a dead tree ahead as if to say, "Come along." The trip back down the mountain was done in silence, the goshawk always moving ahead of Paul, gliding from tree to tree during the descent. Once they arrived at the cabin, the goshawk took up a perch on a low, thick branch in the large maple at the edge of the yard and began preening herself. Paul noted this was the branch where he typically hung game like deer or bear.

"Do I need to do anything for her?" Paul asked.

"No. She'll be fine," said Kimmy.

Paul went inside, tended the fires, and prepared a light lunch. After eating, he stepped outside to see if the goshawk was still on her perch, and she was.

"How will she help us get him?" Paul asked, studying the goshawk from the porch.

"Vanity, Paul. Boncras seethes with it. His vanity will bring him to you, to us. His vanity will undo him. He believes himself to be like a medieval lord. I don't mean this metaphorically. He really does think he is a lord. Boncras tries to hobnob with a group in England called the Old Hawking Club. When he travels in Europe, he makes the rounds of the handful of men still flying hawks. He sees the sport as part of his image."

"How do you know all of this?"

"I worked for him long enough," Kimmy explained. "The man never tired of talking about himself to anyone and everyone. His poor wife once confided in me that he loved his hawks more than he loved her. The man is mad, delusional. I brought the children out once to watch him fly some of birds. I admit it was impressive to see those birds, but to him, everything and everyone is just fuel for his ego."

"The goshawk is bait," Paul said.

"Yes. Boncras is always looking for another bird, willing to pay great sums to get them," Kimmy said. "He buys his birds in Europe because apparently no one here in America practices falconry. Boncras would sometimes bemoan this, saying it was a sign that Americans had no real nobility."

"How do we get His Majesty's attention, then? Bring him to us?" Paul asked.

Over the next week, Paul was busy. Kimmy assured him the goshawk would take care of herself for now, but he would have to make some preparations for the trip to come. Paul began by crafting a glove so that handling the bird would be less painful and look more authentic. Taking a heavy leather work glove— the left hand, Kimmy had advised—Paul stitched a heavy piece of leather to its cuff, creating a gauntlet. Paul was pleased with it after allowing the goshawk to make several landings on it. The goshawk needed no prompting, no enticement to fly to him. There were periods of time when she would disappear but would then return, her talons often bloody from a kill. The goshawk would remain perched on the glove as long as Paul wanted, leaving only when Paul cast her off. Always she would return to her perch in the maple. He would need a way to transport the bird, so Paul fashioned a light container from a large oak pack basket he used for trapping. Cutting one side out and attaching a door with leather hinges and a leather strap and a buckle to fasten it closed, he added a section of broom handle as a perch near the bottom of the converted pack basket. When Paul had completed the carrier, he brought the goshawk to his fist and walked her over to the open container. To his surprise, she deftly stepped from the glove onto the perch in the carrier, turning to face the open door.

"Good girl," Paul said, smiling. "I'm going to close it up now. Don't worry, though, I'll let you right out."

Paul closed the door, fastened the strap, and then stepped back, expecting some form of protest from this wild bird.

"I told you," Kimmy said, "she's here to help. She appreciates your concern, I'm sure."

Paul nodded, unfastened the strap, and opened the door. Seeing that the bird appeared calm and that the enclosure seemed roomy enough, he closed and fastened the door and gently picked up the box. Paul then proceeded to carry the box around the yard. After making a short journey around the perimeter of the yard, Paul sat the box down, opened the door, and offered his gloved hand to the bird. Without hesitation, she stepped onto the glove and roused.

"Good girl," Paul said, smiling broadly.

With that, Paul turned toward the maple, and the goshawk lifted off and took her perch.

"Looks like we're ready," Kimmy said.

The best way to get Thomas Boncras's attention and therefore get him to come back to the United States was through one of his oldest and most trusted servants, a man named Arthur Fowler. From Kimmy's time working at the Boncras estate, she had learned Mr. Fowler was essentially second in command. Mr. Boncras referred to the man as "my gamekeeper" to guests visiting the estate. Arthur was tasked with tending to the property's hunting lands as well as caring for the dogs, horses, and hawks used for hunts. The man was usually in attendance at evening functions as well and seemed to have Mr. Boncras's total confidence. Mr. Fowler was an extension of Boncras's vanity, proof that he was part of the new American nobility. In some ways, Paul and Mr. Fowler were alike. Both men made their living through the hunt, and both depended on the financially well off. The difference in Paul's mind was that while he did on occasion indulge his clients' egos, he had his limits. If the man were as close to Boncras as Kimmy said, the man would almost certainly have been aware of his employer's misdeeds, perhaps even be complicit in them. Paul worried aloud to Kim that his limited knowledge of falconry would be a problem when he communicated with Mr. Fowler. Would the man sense something untoward? But Kimmy allayed his fears.

"Remember, he won't be interested in you so much as the goshawk. If he sees you as a neophyte, a rube, even, so much the better in his eyes. His only goal will be to please his master. That's his ego, his vanity."

It would not be hard to get a message to Mr. Fowler. Whether he were at the New York estate or the hunting lodge in Connecticut, any message sent to him regarding the goshawk would quickly find its way into his hands. Paul would have to spend the next week or so in town so he would be able to send the required messages through the Western Union office. Kimmy was always with Paul, and for him, it was a strange state of being he had ceased questioning. The flow of his destiny was bound to hers by the strength of their love as though he were a leaf being carried on the wind and that wind carrying them both toward a final unification.

The beginning of March brought an unexpected and welcome period of thaw to the land, and although it probably wouldn't last, it had melted enough of the road for Paul to drive his Ford into town. Kimmy assured Paul that the hawk would be there when they returned from their business, and before he got into the vehicle, Paul looked back to see the bird sitting in her familiar perch as if awaiting her orders. Paul and Kimmy did not speak of the tasks ahead of them during the bumpy ride to town, but instead fell into more mundane conversations as though they were still living their old life.

Tom and Margaret were overjoyed to see Paul and were glad when he asked if he might stay with them for a week or so. Paul told them he was getting a bit of cabin fever and thought the unexpected thaw a good opportunity to visit. Margaret, simply glowing with joy at the prospect of having Paul with them for the week, rushed out to buy supplies for the week's meals. Tom and Paul took advantage of the time to catch up. While he was glad that Paul had made such a remarkable turn for the better, Tom still wondered what had made the change possible. Paul had been as low as any man he had ever seen and somehow, he had come out of a state that could only be referred to as despair quite literally overnight. Tom thought it best, however, to keep these questions to himself, lest he inadvertently reverse the progress Paul had made. The two men conversed in the kitchen, Tom bringing Paul up to speed on the goings-on in town and the general news of the past weeks. Upon her return, Margaret shooed the men out of her kitchen and set about cooking dinner.

"It's good for her, you know, having you here," Tom said with a smile, his eyes bright. "I think she gets lonely, just the two of us here. I think she really misses having you visit. She misses you and Kim." When he realized the name he'd mentioned, Tom stopped himself and looked down in shame. "I'm sorry, Paul. I didn't mean to stir things up for you."

"It's okay, Tom. It really is. You can say her name. I'm the one who should be sorry. I've been selfish. You lost her, too. I know how much you both loved her. She loved you both, too." Paul grasped the old man's shoulder lightly. In that moment, Paul had an epiphany and meant what he said. He had not really been able to consider whether the loss had been only his, and although she did not speak to him at the time, Paul could feel Kimmy with them, feel a sadness emanating from her.

The evening was wonderful, the meal a feast, and the three stayed up late drinking coffee and talking, even laughing, in front of the fireplace after dinner. It was the first time since Kimmy's death that the three had reminisced about the young woman who had brought so much joy to their lives. Kimmy did not remain silent to Paul during the evening and took part by bringing up her most treasured memories with them to Paul, which he would then convey. Although Paul alone could hear her, it was as though her joy, her laughter, her love for the three of them permeated the room. It was nearly eleven o'clock when the three decided to turn in, and after good-nights were said, Paul made his way to his room. He settled into the familiar bed, and in whispers, he and Kimmy continued to talk about their memories of Tom and Margaret until Paul drifted off to sleep.

The next morning, after a late breakfast with Tom and Margaret, Paul helped Margaret clean up the kitchen and told the two he felt like a walk in town. Tom had retired to the living room to smoke his pipe and read the paper, and Margaret had already begun preparations for lunch.

"You need some fattening up, Paul," she had said with a wink.

Paul told her he would be back at in time for lunch, that he wouldn't miss it for the world. Tom offered to come along, but Paul told him, too, he would be back soon and to enjoy his paper. Paul walked across town, which was unusually busy because of the thaw, conversing briefly with people he knew along the way. The streets were slushy and muddy in places, and the sky was overcast. Paul arrived at the railroad station and made his way to the Western Union office. A small, nervous-looking, bespectacled man appeared at the window.

"How may I be of service, sir?" the man asked.

"I need to send a telegram," Paul answered.

The man pulled a pen from the counter, produced a small writing pad from beneath, and without looking up, said, "All right. To whom and where?"

"Arthur Fowler, Boncras Estate, Upton, New York," Paul said.

The man copied the information as Paul spoke it, and again without looking up, said, "Proceed, sir."

"Have goshawk. Stop. Flies well. Stop. Would you be interested in purchase? Stop."

"That all?" the man asked, still not looking up.

"That's all," Paul answered.

"And you are?" the man asked, finally glancing up.

"Mr. Miller," Paul said. Miller was his actual surname; Paul had taken to using Thompson instead, as it seemed everyone thought he was Tom and Margaret's child anyway.

"Very good, Mr. Miller. Where would you like the reply to be delivered?" the man asked.

Paul paused. "If it's all the same, I'll come back for it. I'll be out and about for the next few days, hard to find."

"Very well, sir," the little man said. "It will be a couple of days, most likely. Come back then. Let's see, ten words, that will be twenty-five cents, please."

Paul handed the man the money and turned to walk away.

"Oh, sir?" the man called to him. "One more thing."

Paul stopped and turned. "Yes?"

"Thank you for using Western Union," the little man said with a smile.

"Of course. You're welcome," Paul said, continuing on his way.

The next two days were spent happily. Tom and Margaret were happy, and Paul couldn't remember when he had eaten so much. It appeared Margaret's threat to "fatten him up" had not been idle. The topic of conversation with Kimmy had gone from pleasant reminiscence to the more serious future. Paul worried to himself that the plan would not work, and Kimmy's demeanor had turned more stoic. Paul returned to the Western Union office at the appointed day and was disappointed that he had received no reply from Fowler. That night, he expressed his concern to Kimmy.

"Should I send another telegram?"

"No. He'll answer."

Paul thought for a bit, unable to shake his worry. After rolling over in bed, he whispered, "How do you know, Kimmy? We don't even know if he got our message. Maybe we should send another just in case. Aren't you worried?"

"I am beyond worry, Paul. I am beyond fearing what will happen. I only know what must happen. Where is your faith, my love?" Kimmy replied, agitation in her voice.

Paul let it go and tried to sleep. Sleep was fitful, however, and Paul awakened several times during the night, his mind racing. The next morning, Paul made a decision not to visit the Western Union office. He was a hunter. He must think like a hunter. "Patience is among the most deadly of virtues," his father had told him when he was a boy learning to hunt in Western

Pennsylvania. "The hunter who can wait, wait and watch quietly, is the hunter who will make a kill. The prey will always show itself. You just have to outwait it." Paul would wait. This would be his final hunt, and he would have justice. Kimmy, Tom, Margaret, and any others Boncras had hurt or wronged would have it, too.

The next day, Paul arrived at the Western Union office at around eleven o'clock in the morning.

The little man greeted him. "Mr. Miller."

"Sir," Paul replied, nodding to the clerk.

"You have a telegram here, Mr. Miller," the man said, flipping through a stack of telegrams.

"Here it is," said the man, passing the piece of paper to Paul through the window. Paul took the telegram and stepped away from the counter to read it.

Mr. Miller

Need to see goshawk. Can you bring it? Will reimburse travel expenses. At Maple Grove Connecticut estate. Please reply.

Paul was surprised and read the telegram several times.

"The time is close, Paul," Kimmy said.

Paul stepped back up to the window. The little bespectacled man had already gotten his pen and pad ready.

"Do you wish to reply, Mr. Miller?"

"Yes. Thank you. Send this: Will leave tomorrow by train. Stop. Will contact you upon arrival. Stop."

"Got it, Mr. Miller. Ten words, twenty-five cents," the man said.

Paul paid and stood at the window. The man looked at him quizzically for a moment. Then, understanding Paul's prompt, he smiled and said, "Of course, sir, so sorry. Thank you for using Western Union."

With a nod, Paul turned and walked away.

Just around the other side of the station, Paul visited the ticket window and purchased a one-way ticket from Beech Flats, Pennsylvania, to New Canaan, Connecticut, the closest station to the estate at Maple Grove. The trip, with stops along the way would take about four hours, and the train would be leaving Beech Flats at 8:00 a.m., so Paul would arrive at New Canaan around noon. So soon! The enormity that he would be meeting with Mr. Fowler the next day brought the reality of the situation into sharp focus for Paul—one step closer to a meeting with Mr. Boncras. One step closer to killing him. Paul thought of the finality of the statement in his mind. He would kill this man when the opportunity presented itself. It was not fear of the deed he felt, nor doubt that he would do it. Paul would kill him without regret. The memory of Kimmy bruised, beaten, and dead in Parr's basement was fresh in his mind, and he felt a sense of peace, of calm, settling over him, the sense of calm that comes at the end of a stalk when the prey is in one's sights.

Paul placed the train ticket in his coat pocket, and after booking a room at the hotel near the train station, he walked back across town toward Tom and Margaret's. Kimmy was strangely quiet, but Paul could feel her presence. There wasn't much to talk about. It was only a matter of time now, he supposed. Kimmy believed the goshawk would prove irresistible to Boncras and that upon a favorable report from Fowler, he would come straight away. How long would it take him to get back? Paul wondered. It could be weeks if he were traveling from Europe. Paul would stay nearby until the man arrived. He had enough money to rent a room for a few weeks. Paul also thought it possible he would be invited to stay on at the estate until Mr. Boncras arrived. At any rate, the waiting would be the hardest part.

Paul arrived at Tom and Margaret's around noon, and Margaret had lunch ready. During their meal, Paul announced he would be heading back to the cabin afterward to "check on things" and that he would visit at some point in the near future when time allowed. The old couple protested his leaving, but the visit had been so pleasant, the change in Paul's spirits so much better, that they parted company on a positive note. Paul felt some guilt for not being completely honest with them but knew he had no choice.

The temperature had started to drop, and it felt like it could snow at any moment. The sky had that look, and by the time he had traveled about halfway to the cabin, a light snow had begun to fall. Paul arrived at the cabin at around a quarter to two. Paul packed a small suitcase of clothes as well as his game bag, his Solingen knife, and his homemade falconry glove. The goshawk was at her perch, and Paul was pleased to see that her crop was full, indicating she had eaten well that day. That was a good thing, as it meant she should not need to eat for a day or so.

Paul cut a portion of venison off a roast in the icehouse and broke it down further into smaller pieces so he could feed the bird before they boarded the train the next morning. It would be better if the goshawk stayed out of sight of other travelers. The last thing he needed was a bunch of gawkers during the journey. Kimmy's silence had become a concern for Paul. The energy she was putting out was strange, too—well, stranger than it usually was.

"Kimmy?" Paul said quietly. "You there?"

"I'm here, Paul," Kimmy answered, her voice sounding sad.

"Is there something wrong, hon?" Paul asked timidly.

There was a pause; then, Paul heard a whimper, low and mournful, from Kimmy, and then the whimper became sobbing.

"Kimmy, honey," Paul said. "What is it? I'm here. Tell me."

Kimmy continued to sob, the sound full of pain and sadness. Paul let her continue without interruption until, finally, she spoke.

"I'm sorry, Paul," Kimmy sobbed. "I'm so sorry for you, my love. You don't have to do this. You go on with your life. Love again; have children. I don't want you to do this."

Paul was stunned. His heart broke again for his wife. Even in death, even after all that had happened to her, she still thought of his happiness. In truth, the thought of letting go of this had never crossed his mind.

"Don't you say that," Paul began, his voice breaking. "You are everything to me, Kimmy, my heart, my soul. I was so lost without you. We are bound together, and I won't be without you again, no matter what path I have to take. I love you. Don't you know that?"

"I do, Paul," Kimmy answered, crying. "I know you do, and I love you, too."

"What I'm about to do, I'm doing because I want to. Because I have to. No one hurts you and walks away. I'm not afraid, Kimmy. As long as we're together, I'm not afraid to die."

"I love you, Paul," Kimmy said.

"I love you, too, sweetie. Now let's get on with this."

After loading the bird and his meager suitcase into the truck, Paul made the drive back to town and settled into his room at the hotel. The snow had begun to fall in earnest by the time he reached town, and he was glad he had gotten back in front of it. Once in the room, Paul unbuckled the door of the goshawk's carrier and opened the door. The bird roused, stretched, and stood on one leg while holding the other up. The goshawk looked relaxed, and Paul thought it good that at least one of them was. Kimmy was back to being quiet, and the energy around her presence had changed yet again. No longer somber and heavy, it was as if the air around him was charged, crackling like the atmosphere before a big thunderstorm unleashes itself.

Paul felt, inside of himself, not fear or nervousness, but a sense of restlessness, an anxious desire for action after his long ordeal. Needing to bleed off some of this energy, Paul went downstairs to the restaurant and ate—he was hungrier than he'd expected—and then went outside to pace the porch. Paul would have liked to have taken a proper walk, but he was worried about running into Tom or Margaret. As unlikely as that possibility may have been, Paul felt no desire to explain his presence in town with lies.

"Paul, are you okay?" Kimmy asked as he paced the porch.

"Yes, I'm fine. Just a bit anxious," Paul answered. "And you?"

"Anxious. But ready."

Paul paced a while longer; then, after returning to his room, he looked in on the goshawk, who, with the exception of changing legs, was holding steady. Paul opened his suitcase and retrieved his knife and his small sharpening kit. The kit consisted of three stones and a small bottle of oil in a compact canvas roll with pockets for each of the components. Paul unrolled the case on the writing desk next to his bed and unsheathed the Solingen, placing the sheath out of the way on the right side of the desk. The knife was a big one with a seven-inch blade and stag handle. The blade, while clean, bore the stains of much use. Using his thumb, Paul tested the edge, and while it felt sharp, he knew it could be sharper. Selecting the finest grit stone from its pocket, Paul placed several drops of the oil on it and spread it evenly across the stone's surface with his fingers. Paul then began to hone the blade, drawing the edge across the oiled stone as though he were trying to cut off thin slices of it, an equal number of strokes for each side of the edge. As Paul worked on the knife, he imagined what someone would think if they were to walk in on this scene, a man with a goshawk in a hotel room sharpening a large hunting knife while occasionally talking to himself—nothing sinister here at all. When he voiced his thoughts to Kimmy, they both had a much-needed moment of levity. The goshawk continued being itself, seemingly above it all.

Paul slept surprisingly well that night and awakened around 6:00 a.m. After washing and shaving, Paul took out the package of venison and unwrapped it, put on his glove, and fed the bird. The goshawk's appetite was undiminished by its strange surroundings, and it ate greedily, consuming the entire package in short order. The bird cropped up, it wiped its beak on the carrier's perch, roused, and settled back in. Paul went downstairs and ate a small breakfast of toast and over-easy eggs and stepped outside onto the porch. The snow had ended, but in the night, several inches had accumulated.

Paul returned to the room, packed his belongings into the suitcase, and closed the goshawk's carrier. After making a final survey of the room to ensure he had left nothing behind, he made his way downstairs, returned his room key, and exited the hotel. It took only a moment to walk across the street to the station, and Tom found it thankfully sparse as far as people were concerned. Paul checked his watch. It was only a quarter after seven, and he had some time to wait, so he took a seat on one of the platform's benches. Although he could have waited inside, Paul preferred the bracing air and the privacy of the platform where he could converse openly with Kimmy. Although her energy remained volatile, they managed to reminisce about their first train ride together while they waited for the train. The upcoming journey and the train that would take them on it had unconsciously become a symbol of the beginning of the end to Paul, the end of his quest for justice, the end of his separation from his wife, and the end of Thomas Boncras.

At about ten till eight, the train pulled into the station. A few passengers disembarked, and Paul, along with four other passengers, boarded. After the conductor punched his ticket, Paul had a seat, placing the hawk's carrier on the seat next to him. The car was mostly vacant, and the fellow passengers appeared to pay him no mind. At five after eight, the train got under way, and Paul soon lost himself in the scenery rushing by—farms, homes, and stretches of forest—as they passed through the mountains. The train made its stops at small towns like Newfoundland, Pennsylvania, and Milford, New York, but because passengers were getting off and on at these stops, the number of passengers in the car remained relatively unchanged, and no one asked him what was in the container. It struck Paul that most people saw little of the workings of the world around them, being so absorbed in their own interests. How many times had he considered the lives, interests, and trials of the people he'd passed on the streets? Not often. Probably never, he mused. How many had he passed in his life who might have been as burdened by grief or worry as he had been?

About two hours into the trip, Paul decided he had better check on the goshawk. Kimmy told him she was fine, but Paul had to see for himself. It seemed to him highly unhealthy for such a wild creature to be confined like this. Paul looked around the car, and, satisfied that the other passengers were not paying attention, he unbuckled the strap and pulled the door open about an inch to take a look inside. The goshawk was perched on one leg and looked relaxed and well. As Paul regarded the bird, it looked at him and tilted its head to one side, looking curious as to the purpose of the intrusion. Paul smiled to himself, closed the door, and fastened the buckle.

At around noon, as scheduled, the train rolled into the station at North Canaan. Paul picked up the carrier and his suitcase, and along with four other travelers, stepped off the train. Once on the platform, Paul considered how to get word to the estate that he had arrived. Perhaps he could place a call from the station. As the other passengers went on their way, Paul noticed a man standing at the other side of the platform.

"Fowler's here, Paul," Kimmy hissed. "That's him."

The man was an average height and build, wearing a forest-green jacket, wool pants, a wool-tweed newsboy hat, and tall, lace-up hunting boots. The man approached Paul, looking him over carefully. Paul likewise surveyed Mr. Fowler.

"Mr. Fowler," Paul said, putting down the carrier and extending his right hand.

"Ah, Mr. Miller," Fowler said with a thin smile, shaking Paul's hand. "I took the liberty of coming down here to meet you, Mr. Miller," Fowler said. "Wasn't entirely sure you'd be here, but this is the only train, and checking the schedule, I assumed you'd be here."

"Thank you so much," Paul said. "That was very courteous of you."

"Is that the bird?" Fowler asked, pointing at the carrier.

"It is," Paul answered.

"That is quite ingenious, that carrier you have there. Is that a pack basket?" Fowler asked, smiling.

"It is. It works well," Paul answered, picking up the carrier.

"Quite inventive. I've never seen anything like it." Fowler motioned for Paul to follow him. "The car is parked around the front."

The two men walked to the front of the station where the car sat idling. The uniformed driver got out of the car and approached the men.

"Take your luggage, sir?" the driver asked.

"No, thank you," Paul said, shaking his head. "I don't have much."

"Very well, sir." The driver moved ahead of the two men and opened the car door. Paul entered first and had a seat. The car was very roomy, so Paul placed the carrier on the seat to his left side. Once Fowler had taken his seat in the back with Paul, the driver got them underway.

"Took a chance coming out to meet you, as I said," Fowler began. "I've never had someone contact me about a bird. Not here in the States, anyway. To be honest, I was excited to see if you were the real deal."

Paul didn't respond but instead nodded his assent.

"I'm sure you know that falconry isn't an American pastime. It's barely practiced in Europe these days. How did you become acquainted with the sport, Mr. Miller?"

"I'm not what you would call acquainted with the sport. I don't really know much. I got the goshawk as a chick. Found her in the woods. I fed her, raised her up, and it just went on from there," Paul said, feeling awkward in the lie.

Mr. Fowler looked at Paul thoughtfully, and then out the passenger window, and then back at Paul. Paul wondered if he had said something he shouldn't have. A smile appeared on Fowler's face. "You mean to tell me that you found this bird in the forest as an eyas—that's what you call a nestling hawk—and you simply raised her and picked up the flying naturally? I mean, I don't know what to say. That's extraordinary, Mr. Miller! Just extraordinary! I'm very excited to see her," Fowler said, a look of wonder on his face.

The drive to the estate was brief, the big Rolls covering the five miles in no time. They entered the estate through an ornate wrought-iron gate manned by two uniformed staff. The estate seemed sizable. From the point of entry, there were no dwellings to be seen.

"He's here, Paul. Boncras is here!" Kimmy exclaimed.

Paul, being unable to respond, waited for her to elaborate on her statement.

"I feel it. The man is here. He's not in Europe, after all. Be ready. Be careful. I love you."

Paul gave an abbreviated nod, the only response he could give in the company of Fowler. The car ascended the slowly rising road, which turned to the right at the top of the small rise. The estate was heavily wooded until the crest of the rise. At this vantage point, Paul could see a large open space of meadows and cut cornfields. At the far end of the open ground, which Paul estimated at about thirty acres, Paul could see a large, stately house flanked by what appeared to be barns of some sort. The road hugged the right edge of the fields, which were bordered by oak, beech, maple, and other hardwoods.

The estate house was set up much like a traditional English manor, with extensive hedges around the grounds. A gravel drive terminated in a roundabout at the entrance, with the graveled road branching off to the left and right, leading off to the large, brick, barnlike structures set about a hundred yards to either side of the mansion. The car pulled into the roundabout and circled around to the front before coming to a stop.

The driver shut down the engine and came around to get the doors. As Paul exited the car, he could see a man in a red woolen coat holding two bird dogs on leashes. Fowler came around the car and, motioning for Paul to follow him, walked up to the man with the dogs.

"This is Michael. Michael helps around the grounds, takes care of the dogs, et cetera," Fowler said, presenting the man. "This is Mr. Miller, Michael."

"Pleased to meet you, sir," said Michael, extending his hand.

"Likewise, Michael," Paul said, grasping the man's hand and shaking it.

Mr. Fowler stepped up to Paul and placed his hand on his shoulder. "I know it's horribly rude of me—you must be tired and hungry—but I really must see this bird. If you would indulge me, I promise a very memorable lunch," Fowler said, smiling.

"Of course," Paul replied. "It's not rude at all. That's why I'm here."

"Wonderful! Just wonderful!" Fowler said. Then he turned to Michael. "Please set some birds up in the second cornfield for us, would you? I'll take the dogs from here. Thank you."

Michael nodded and turned the leashes over to Fowler, who began to absentmindedly pet the dogs.

"We raise quail and pheasant on the estate, you see. Mr. Miller, please make whatever preparations you need for the bird, and let's get a look at her," Fowler said.

Paul nodded, turned, and set the carrier and his suitcase on the gravel drive. It was happening quickly. Paul had no idea when he would meet Boncras, but he needed to be ready if an opportunity presented itself. Opening the suitcase, Paul removed his game bag and hung it over his neck and shoulders, the bag resting on his right hip. Still facing away from Fowler, Paul opened the bag, which contained two items: his glove and his knife. He reached in and deftly unsheathed the big knife, leaving it loose in the heavy leather bag. He needed to be able to get to the knife quickly when the time came. He then removed the glove, placed it on his left hand, closed the flap of the game bag, and, kneeling, closed the suitcase. Still kneeling, Paul undid the buckle on the door strap of the carrier and opened the door. The goshawk roused. Paul offered his gloved hand, and the bird stepped up without further prompting.

"Remarkable! Just amazing!" Paul heard a voice from in front of him exclaim.

Looking up, he saw a large, heavyset man standing in front of him. The man looked to be about fifty or so, with dark hair and a prominent moustache, and he was dressed in fashionable hunting garb.

"It's him, Paul!" Kimmy said, her energy crackling.

Paul stood and faced the man. This was Boncras. This was the man who had brutalized his wife, beaten her to death, and left her in the snow. Every part of Paul cried out to kill the man, but the hunter in him whispered for him to be patient. Paul had to be sure he would not be stopped, that he had a clear kill. He would wait.

"Mr. Boncras!" Fowler said, coming around between the men. "This is Mr. Miller, the man I told you about, and the goshawk. Mr. Miller, may I present Mr. Thomas Boncras?"

"A pleasure, Mr. Miller. Such a delight, really," said Boncras, taking Paul's right hand in a firm handshake.

"You're too kind, sir. The pleasure is mine," Paul said, feeling queasy and wanting the man to release his hand.

Boncras finally let go and regarded the bird. After a brief examination, Boncras looked at Fowler and then back at Paul. He raised his eyebrows and said, "No jesses of any kind! Do you see that, man? And no hood? Just astonishing. How do you manage her, sir?" Boncras asked with genuine curiosity.

"She trusts me, sir. I don't even know what jesses are, to be truthful. We've just done it this way," Paul answered hesitantly.

There was an exchange of astounded glances between Fowler and Boncras.

"I've never even heard of such a thing," said Fowler, shaking his head. "Didn't even know it was possible."

"It is something, to be sure," Boncras agreed. "Let us see how she does on some pheasant. How would that be, Mr. Miller? Will she be agreeable to us in the field with her?" he asked.

"Of course. No problem, sir," Paul answered.

"Very well, then. Lead on, Arthur!" Mr. Boncras said excitedly.

The men started forward, Fowler about twenty paces ahead with the dogs and Mr. Boncras walking with him on his right side. The sky was slightly overcast with no wind, the clouds overhead sometimes breaking to let in a beam of sunshine. The men left the immediate grounds surrounding the house and walked across an unmown field of grass. Paul had been on many bird hunts, and to him, it seemed the setup was the same with a hawk as it was with a shotgun, the dogs a bit ahead and the shooter— or the bird, in this case—staying a bit back. It took some time to cross the first field, and once they entered the cut cornfield, Fowler unclipped the dogs, and they bounded enthusiastically ahead, seeking out the pheasant, which had earlier been released by Michael. It wasn't long before the dogs went to point in the corn stubble, looking like quivering statues. Fowler glanced back at Paul. The goshawk had begun to pitch slightly forward on the glove as if she were winding up. Paul nodded at Fowler. At his signal, the dogs flushed the bird, a big cock pheasant, which exploded upward. The goshawk was off his fist before he knew it, pumping its wings in powerful beats, gaining speed. The pheasant pitched forward in flight but made it only about fifty yards before the big goshawk slammed into him and brought him to the ground.

"Splendid! Bravo!" cried Boncras, looking like an exited child.

The goshawk was mantled on top of the pheasant, footing it, driving those needle-sharp talons deep into its body. Fowler was calling the dogs back, and Boncras stared as if mesmerized at the scene in front of him.

Paul's hand deftly retrieved the razor-sharp Solingen from the game bag, and stepping slightly behind Boncras, grabbed the man by the left shoulder and drew the blade quickly across the back of his thighs, hamstringing him. Boncras gave out a grunt as Paul then plunged the blade into his side. The man was squealing like a rabbit caught by a fox as he went down, clutching at the wound in his right side. Fowler looked back in time to see his master drop to his knees, Paul stepping in front of him, the big knife in his hand.

"Sir!" Fowler cried, beginning to sprint toward the two men. The dogs, seeming to sense what was happening, fled the field, whining with their tails between their legs. Fowler had about fifty yards to cover, and he had covered only ten of them when the goshawk, which had left its kill, closed the distance to the man and bound itself to the left side of his face. Crying out in pain, Fowler clutched at the great bird, trying to free himself.

The goshawk, with lightning speed, briefly released the man, gained a few feet of altitude above him, and dove back at his face. The goshawk in short order blinded Fowler and took to the air. He fell to the ground clutching his face, his mangled right eye dislodged from its socket and resting on his bloody cheek.

Satisfied that he would not be stopped, Paul focused his attention on Boncras. Paul could feel Kimmy all around them like a storm.

"Kimberly Thompson. You killed her. She was my wife," Paul said coldly.

Boncras said nothing. The man looked surprised and confused. Tears rolled down his cheeks. Paul grabbed a handful of the man's hair and pushed his head backward, exposing his throat. In the background, Paul could hear Fowler's cries of pain. Paul placed the knife against the left of Boncras's neck, preparing to strike, and Boncras began to scream, a scream of absolute terror, but it was not the knife, not Paul that he saw in his final moment. In the moment before the blade cut his throat, Boncras saw Kimmy in front of him. Beautiful. Terrible. Kimmy stood before him an avenging angel, anger burning in her blazing eyes.

"This is my justice. God's justice!" she screamed.

They were the last words Boncras heard, Kimmy the last thing he saw. Paul drew the blade firmly and quickly across the man's throat. Blood poured from the incision, which was so deep, the man was nearly decapitated. Paul held the man's head up for a brief moment and watched the life leave his eyes before releasing him and letting his body fall to ground.

As Paul stood over Boncras's body, he caught something to his left in his peripheral vision. Paul, thinking it must be the other servant, the one named Michael, turned quickly toward the perceived threat, knife at the ready. Paul was stunned. Standing before him was Kimmy.

"Paul," she said, pointing to where Fowler was writhing in agony. Paul took a moment to look at her. She was beautiful, but her eyes were filled with tears. Without a word, Paul turned and walked over to Fowler. Fowler rolled into Paul's leg and grasped his boot.

"Please," Fowler begged, "Please, sir, help me. Have mercy. I'm blind."

"The same mercy you and Boncras showed all of those women?" Paul asked. "That kind of mercy?"

"I didn't hurt any of them…never touched them till after. He made me help him. I had no choice," Fowler stuttered.

It was true then that Fowler had been complicit in Boncras's crimes.

"I have no choice, either," Paul said. He stepped around Fowler, straddled the man's body, reached down, grabbed him by the hair, and slit his throat. After the cut, Paul released the man's limp head, dropped the knife, and stepped away toward the spot where Kimmy was standing. Behind him, he could hear Fowler's last death rattles.

"It's over, Kimmy," Paul said, reaching out to her with his bloody right hand. "Let's leave this place. I'm sorry for what happened to you."

Kimmy reached out and took his hand. Paul felt only a warm energy from her grasp like the sun, and a surprised look came across his face.

"Soon we'll be truly joined, Paul. Don't worry." Kimmy was smiling. The two of them walked away from the estate, crossing the other fields of grass and corn stubble. If they had looked back, they would have seen Michael slowly, tentatively making his way across the field behind them, toward the bodies. Michael had seen it all happen from the tree line but had stayed back. After surveying the grisly scene, Michael thought it prudent not to pursue the man walking slowly away in the distance, but instead ran back to the main house to summon the authorities by phone.

Paul and Kimmy made their way out to the main road and began walking back toward North Canaan. As they walked, they spoke little, Paul beginning to feel the enormity of taking two men's lives. While he did not regret killing them, he felt a sense of shock all the same. The police took Paul into custody along the road without incident, and as Paul was covered in blood, it was not difficult for them to discern he was their man. The officers were puzzled when Paul began to have a conversation with himself during the drive back to North Canaan but assumed they were the ravings of a troubled mind and left it at that.

There would be no trial as Paul pled guilty to the crime and was sentenced to death. Tom and Margaret came to see him one last time after he was moved to the state prison at Wethersfield. Tom was stoic about what had happened and was proud that Paul had honored Kimmy, but it saddened him deeply that he would lose Paul. Margaret, upon seeing Paul, cried inconsolably, and Tom had to cut the visit shorter than he had intended. Paul asked that neither of them attend the execution, as it would only serve to upset them further, and instead asked them to remember him and Kimmy as they had been in happier times.

The "Hawk Murders," as they were dubbed by the press, gained the public's interest for a time, owing mostly to Michael's account of what he had seen in the field that day. The idea that the hawk and the man had worked together to kill his colleagues, one of them somewhat prominent, captured the public's attention until the trial of Gerald Chapman started. Mr. Chapman, or the "Count of Gramercy Park," as he was sometimes called, had murdered Officer James Skelly of the New Britain police department back in 1924 and was finally apprehended in Indiana in January 1925. With the additional title of "Public Enemy Number One," the public soon forgot about Paul and the "Hawk Murders" and focused on the dashing Chapman.

One reporter from the *Hartford Testament* took an interest in Paul and the murders and visited Paul with some frequency. The reporter was fascinated by the details of Paul's story, which Paul, having nothing to lose, told with complete honesty. Initially, the reporter thought Paul insane, and the guards' stories of Paul holding conversations with "Kimmy" seemed to confirm this idea. The more the reporter looked into the case, however, the more he began to believe Paul's improbable story. He traveled to Parrs' and attempted to interview the elder Parr, but the man entered a state of terror at the mention of the alleged incident in the basement and asked the reporter that he leave and never return. It was clear to the reporter that something had happened.

The reporter had also paid a visit to Tom and Margaret, and while Margaret was too upset to speak with him, Tom was more than happy to fill the newspaper man in on the troubling circumstances surrounding Boncras in general and his probable involvement in Kimmy's murder. Tom had gone a step further and referred the man to a few of his old Pinkerton contacts in New York. The reporter found that while none of the men would allow him to quote them as they had no solid proof, all were convinced that Mr. Boncras was responsible for murdering Paul's wife and that an innocent man had taken the fall for it. The local police who had worked the case and made the arrest would not comment except to say that justice had been served in the matter. It was clear to the reporter that the Boncras family still had great sway.

None of these things would appear in the *Hartford Testament.* None of it could really be substantiated, and it would have to do that the reporter alone had come to believe Paul's tale of murder, a cover-up, a vengeful ghost, a mysterious intervention by a bird, and bloody justice meted out to the guilty.

Paul was scheduled for execution on May 16, and the reporter had asked Paul if he might attend. Paul had no objections and surprisingly none to the reporter's additional request that he be permitted to take a few photographs for the paper. The reporter would later write that he had seen few men as happy or as carefree as Paul. The man's circumstances would seem to have prohibited such joy, but the reporter wrote in explanation, "Paul Miller appears to have no fear of death, believing as he does that upon the end of his Earthly life, he will be immediately reunited with his lost love. Indeed, even as I converse with the man, he sometimes breaks into conversation with someone he believes to be his deceased wife, Kimberly. The guards I have spoken to concerning the prisoner likewise speak of his congeniality and his somewhat constant conversation with his departed wife."

Paul was to be executed by hanging, but not the typical method of dropping from a gallows. A new, reportedly more humane method of hanging had been developed and had been adopted by Connecticut. The new method was known as the "Upright Jerker." The upright jerker was, as the name implied, a method of execution by hanging which jerked the subject violently upward by means of a three-hundred-pound counter-weight. The noose was attached via cables and pulleys. Advocates of this method believed it to be superior to the old method of dropping the condemned in that the sudden and intense upward movement of the noose was more prone to break the person's neck and cause immediate dispatch. However, the method had proven to be about as hit or miss in regards to immediate dis-patch as the older method—some of the condemned took a bit of time to expire after being snatched into the air and swung about wildly while slowly strangling.

The apparatus had been installed in an enclosed outdoor area to the rear of the main prison, a sort of courtyard. The device would later be reinstalled in an interior space within the Wethersfield facility. The morning of the execution was one of those glorious spring mornings, warm and bright. Besides the reporter, only two other people, Thomas Boncras's parents, were in attendance. The usual prison retinue was on hand for the event, including a minister and a medical doctor. At five minutes till eleven in the morning, Paul was walked to the spot marked on the pavement. Above this spot dangled a noose of hemp rope attached to a steel cable.

Paul's demeanor belied the fact that he would momentarily be hanging from the noose that dangled within a foot of where he stood. While not smiling, Paul nonetheless had a pleasant, content look on his face, a look of peace. Boncras's parents refrained from looking the man in the eyes, so great was his look of peace. The reporter noticed this and wondered to himself if their inability to face the man who had killed their son was an indication of some knowledge on their part of the type of man Thomas had been. How much had the two of them really known of their son's behaviors and misdeeds? It was impossible to prove conclusively, but it seemed improbable to the reporter that Thomas Boncras's parents were in the dark about the true nature of their son.

Once Paul was in the designated spot, he was joined by the minister. The two said a short prayer, and then the minister asked him if he had any final words. Paul nodded in assent and spoke, directing his gaze and words to the Boncrases.

"I am sorry for the pain you must be feeling for the loss of your son. I am not sorry, however, for what I did, being justified by the evil your son visited upon my wife, Kimmy, and I am ready to face almighty God with a clear conscience for my deeds."

While the Boncrases said nothing, Mr. Boncras looked as if he had been slapped and cast an angry gaze upon the warden. The warden reacted to the man's look by nodding impatiently at the minister, who quietly took his leave of the area. Upon the minister's departure, a pair of guards approached Paul. One of the guards carried a hood made of dark fabric in his right hand, the other a document of some kind. Once the two were in positions flanking Paul, the man carrying the document cleared his throat and began to read it.

"Paul Miller, you have been convicted of the crime of murder by the State of Connecticut and sentenced to death by hanging on this day, May 16, 1925. May God have mercy on your soul."

With the document read, the guard folded the paper, placed it in his coat pocket, and took Paul by the left arm while his fellow guard deftly slipped the hood over Paul's head.

"I'm here, Paul," Kimmy said sweetly. "Don't be afraid."

Once the hood was in place, the noose was put around Paul's neck, the rope tightened and positioned behind his right ear. Both guards maintained a firm grip on him during the process and only stepped away a moment before the warden nodded to some unseen individual.

During this time, the reporter took a series of photos of the events leading up to the hanging with his Kodak No. 1 Autographic camera. With the moment of truth at hand, the reporter had steadied himself over a chair back, hoping to catch the split second in which Paul Miller would be pulled skyward by the counterweight. With the subtle nod from the warden, Paul was yanked violently upward. The reporter, surprised by the speed of the act, took his photo a moment late and frantically reset the camera for another shot. Strangely enough, the reporter was sure he had heard the crack of Paul's neck being broken as the contraption was released, despite the chaos of the moment. Camera ready, the reporter waited for Paul's body to cease bouncing and took a final photograph.

In the moments after Paul's body ceased its dance, the silence was heavy and overwhelming. The reporter would write, "As Paul Miller's body came to rest at the end of the rope, it was as if the world stopped for a moment, so heavy and complete was the quiet. To my ears, not even the chirp of the birds was discernible."

Paul's body was shipped back to Beech Flats the next day, where it was received by Tom and one of the Parr sons at the station. The incident during Kimmy's preparation still fresh in his mind, the elder Parr left the work on Paul to his sons. Paul was laid to rest next to his beloved wife in a modest ceremony attended only by Margaret, Tom, and—if one would have looked closely at the tree line beyond the cemetery—the goshawk.

Meanwhile, in Hartford, the reporter who had spent so much time with Paul during his incarceration was finishing up his piece on the Hawk Murders. The reporter was disappointed that so much of what Paul Miller had shared with him would never find its way to print. The editors had forbidden it, citing the scurrilous and unfounded nature of Paul's accusations against Boncras and the undoubted reach the family possessed. The reporter understood his editor's reticence, though he personally believed all of what Paul had told him. This belief was further buoyed by another seeming disappointment connected to the story. After processing the roll of film used to photograph the execution, the reporter found none of the finished prints suitable for publication. All of the photos of Paul, those of him in the moments before and after his death, appeared smudged, a misty-white haze obscuring a clear view of the condemned man. None of the prints would be of use for publication, the reporter agreed, but as with so much else in this story, the reporter had his own opinions. These opinions, like his others, would be kept to himself. The misty-white haze visible in the photos leading up to Paul Miller's death looked to the reporter to be in the shape of a figure, a female figure. The female figure seemed to be embracing Paul as he was prepared for execution. The final photo, the one of Paul hanging lifeless, showed not one misty figure but two, one female and one male, in an embrace, the figures caught at that moment in time hovering as if ascending above the dangling body.

COAXER

In his small, conservatively decorated office, the doctor was taking notes, transcribing information from a book to a yellow legal pad. He was a doctor of psychiatry specializing in hypnotherapy. The man had been in practice for many years, was well established and respected by his peers, and had successfully treated patients with a variety of maladies.

The doctor had been fixated, however, even obsessed, by an idea that had come to him in the past months. The idea fell well outside of the moral and ethical bounds of his profession, and he had at first been able to see it as a novel thought, a whimsy. He was not sure when the idea had left the realm of thought and had become action, but as he took notes, an inner part of him had committed itself to bringing the idea to fruition. In truth, he knew he would only be *trying* to. After all, it was just theoretical, wasn't it?

An object in motion, he continued his notes:

"Weighted Core Experience Index," Dr. Ring, 1980

1. An experience of peace and well-being, and an absence of pain.
2. A sense of detachment from the physical body, progressing to an out-of-body experience.
3. Entering darkness, a tunnel experience with panoramic memory and predominantly positive effects.
4. An experience of a light that is bright, warm, and attractive.
5. Entering the light; meeting persons or figures.

After finishing these notes, the doctor marked his place in the book with a Post-it note, placed it on his desk, and picked up a second book. After leafing through the book and finding what he was looking for, the doctor laid the book on his desk and resumed his note-taking.

"The Greyson Scale," Dr. Greyson, 1983

1. Entering an altered state of time.
2. Experiencing accelerated thought processes.
3. Life review.
4. Sense of sudden understanding.
5. Feelings of peace.
6. Feelings of joy.
7. Feelings of cosmic oneness.
8. Seeing/feeling surrounded by light.
9. Having vivid sensations.
10. Extrasensory perceptions.
11. Experiencing visions.

12. Experiencing a sense of being outside of the physical body.
13. Experiencing a sense of an "otherworldly" environment.
14. Experiencing a sense of a mystical entity.
15. Experiencing a sense of deceased/religious figures.
16. Experiencing a sense of a border, or a point of no return.

Once the doctor had taken these notes, he began thinking about how to proceed. The criteria for the experiences were rather straightforward, and some of the criteria were already part of scenarios or scripts he used in his hypnotic sessions. The rest, he surmised, would be simple to add onto a session.

The criteria given on the Weighted Core Experience Index and the Greyson Scale had been developed to grade and assess "near-death" experiences, or NDEs, as opposed to "other" experiences in patients who had flatlined during medical emergencies, resulting in cardiac arrest. In truth, cardiac arrest was the causal mechanism for all death.

Therefore, he concluded the medical side of the equation would be his goal. He would be putting the cart ahead of the horse, as it were. The doctor had often mused in wonder at the power of the mind, the subconscious mind in particular. How much of our decision-making could we actually ascribe to the logic of the conscious mind? Very little, he had concluded. Most of the decisions we deem to be logical and analytical were at the least colored by, and at most totally dictated by, our subconscious desires and fears.

Even the nature of the mind had not been fully explained. The ideas related to the mind, such as consciousness, reality, and thought, were all just theoretical, and as such gave wide latitude for philosophy, religion, and science to try their hands at explaining it. All had fallen short of the point where theory departed and fact began. The doctor was not sure himself where his experiment would fall within this debate, and in many ways, it was of no consequence to him.

Of one thing, the doctor was sure. What he was going to do, or attempt to do, fell well outside of the moral and ethical bounds of his profession. This much was clear to him. Knowing this, the doctor had decreed he would proceed anyway. What did that make him? Was he a monster without empathy for his patients? Perhaps.

A part of the doctor tried to justify what he had planned as the inexorable march of learning, of science, but the realist in him knew better. It was doubtful there would be any great questions answered, whatever the outcome. Without hard empirical evidence, a metric with which to measure data, the whole thing would be somewhat anecdotal. Maybe the doctor was doing it for one of the oldest of man's reasons—because he could. Of course, doing it, performing the act, did not mean that anything would necessarily happen. But he had resolved to see.

The doctor, after looking over the criteria laid out in the Weighted Core Experience Index and the Greyson Scale, concluded he would use the criteria of the latter. There was redundancy between the two, but the doctor felt the criteria of "The Greyson Scale" to be more detailed. The doctor had learned that the criteria of the scale had been scored, and that a minimum score of seven was required for an experience to be defined as an

NDE. That presented no problems for the doctor's purposes; he would be sure to provide the subject with what he thought were more than enough of the criteria to qualify.

In choosing a patient, the doctor would have to be discerning. The doctor devised some criteria of his own. The purposes of the criteria were twofold: first to provide a subject that would be as neutral as possible as far as religious belief and state of health, and second, a subject who would not arouse suspicion if the experiment bore the fruit he was hoping for. To these ends, the doctor returned to his note taking, and turning a fresh sheet on his legal pad, wrote the following notes.

Subject criteria:

Subject should be over sixty years of age, with a preference, all other things being more or less equal, for those oldest.

Subject should be of relatively good overall health with no history of heart disease, diabetes, or cancer.

Subject should be single, with a preference to those who have little or no immediate family living in the area.

Ideal subject would be retired, with no strong ties to the community in which he or she lives.

Ideal subject would be a long-term patient (a year or more).

Subject should hold no deep religious convictions—an atheist or agnostic is ideal.

After looking over his newly written criteria, the doctor stood and walked to his filing cabinet, opened the top of the three drawers, and began browsing through the files of his current patients. The doctor had had several in mind from the start, so he pulled those files first, placed them on his desk, and then returned to the filing cabinet, carefully looking over the rest of the files.

After almost two hours of poring over records, the doctor had accrued eleven patients who appeared to meet the criteria. Out of the eleven possible subjects, the doctor continued to gravitate toward one. The patient, a sixty-six-year-old woman named Tessa, had been a longtime patient of the doctor's. He had worked with her for well over ten years, and as he looked over her session notes, he noticed that beyond satisfying the other criteria he had laid out, the woman appeared to be exceptionally susceptible to hypnosis. As a matter of fact, the bulk of her sessions for the past four years had been hypnosis sessions.

It seemed after getting a handle on her almost debilitating anxiety, Tessa had found it useful to meet with the doctor every couple of weeks or so to get a hypnotic "booster shot." The sessions generally involved maintaining or deepening her sense of calm and well-being. Perfect. Tessa was perfect. She had the proclivity to "go down," as they say, deeply and smoothly into a hypnotic state. The session he had in mind could be easily evolved out of one of Tessa's usual sessions. At any rate, she wouldn't ever be consciously aware of the changes, anyway, whether the session was successful or not.

The doctor picked up his phone and checked his calendar. Tessa, as fate would have it, was scheduled for her next session the following Thursday. It was Sunday, so the doctor had but four days to wait. Waiting could be difficult, as would be working with other patients. He knew that, by nature, he would be fixating on the upcoming session with Tessa and would find it hard to be present during these other sessions. After a few moments of thought, the doctor pushed the intercom button on his desk phone, hit Line 2, and spoke.

"Carol?" the doctor said.

"Yes, Doctor, what can I do for you?" the receptionist answered.

"Please clear my upcoming schedule until Thursday," the doctor instructed. "I'll be taking a few days. Reschedule them at our earliest openings, please."

"Will do," said Carol. She added, "Is everything okay?"

The doctor paused for a moment before answering, caught off guard by the inquiry into his well-being.

"Oh. Sure, Carol; everything's fine. Just need to take a few days to recharge the old batteries," he replied jovially.

"Good. I know exactly what you mean."

"Thanks, Carol." Before Carol could add anything, the doctor pushed the blinking Line 2 button and ended the conversation.

The doctor spent the next few days working the script for the upcoming session with Tessa and diverting his nervous energy into thoughtless pursuits like going to the movies, eating out, and shopping. The doctor could not remember a period in his life where he had seen so many movies back-to-back at a theater and lamented that, for the most part, the productions were a disappointment. However, they did help consume the time that lay between him and his upcoming experiment. The doctor tried to spend as little time home as possible. Knowing his own nature, he would likely obsess over the upcoming session with Tessa.

Even with his unplanned schedule of theaters, restaurants, and shops, he caught himself thinking ahead. The doctor would have described his mental state about the issue as anxious, but not fearful. He knew that however it worked out, there was little to no risk of repercussion, and the idea was exciting to him. Excitement itself was exciting to him after living a life of such routine normality. The doctor wondered if he would be able to go back to his old, predictable life in the aftermath of this endeavor.

The most obvious answer was no. Even if he failed, he mused, there would be other things to try. The frontier of the mind was infinite, as was his unleashed desire to explore it. Like a child with a chemistry set, the doctor had exciting possibilities in his grasp, and it had been many years since he had been excited about anything. He doubted he would revert back to the old monotony.

The day of the "experiment" arrived, and the doctor awoke excited, but at the same time, somehow subdued. He dressed, made coffee, prepared a simple breakfast of scrambled eggs and toast, and after having his breakfast and coffee, drove his old but serviceable Subaru to his office. It occurred to him that routine was very important. In following an established routine, one finds order and safety. A lot can be hidden, *is* hidden, in the safety of order and routine, he surmised. He had seen it time and time again in his patients' lives. Affairs, phobias, manias, et cetera— virtually anything can be hidden within the shroud of routine.

After ruminating on the nature and possibility of routine, the doctor surmised that his routine, the rhythm of his life, was thick enough to shield him from any scrutiny.

After parking his car in its spot in the parking garage, the same spot he had used for years, the doctor walked the half block to his office. It was a strange sensation to feel butterflies in his stomach. It was a sensation he had not felt since he was very young. The doctor recalled it was during his courtship with his wife that he last remembered feeling butterflies in his stomach.

The memory of his wife brought out a sense of sadness in the doctor. She had been diagnosed with lymphoma eleven years into their marriage and had died before their twelfth anniversary. After a time of intense grieving, he had thrown himself into his work and routine to cope with the loss and loneliness. As the doctor neared his building, he wondered to himself if part of this obsession with the "experiment," as he referred to it, was connected to the loss of his wife. Did he have a deep-seated need to know, to get an inkling of whether or not his wife had "moved on" in some way? In his therapist's mind, he thought it possible his subconscious was acting on his grief, but his conscious, logical mind wasn't sure. At this point, as with most compulsions he felt, he was on autopilot, moving inexorably toward the moment when the deed was done.

After entering the building, the doctor took the elevator to the third floor, and upon exiting it, turned left and walked down the hall. His office was the last one on the right, and on the way, the doctor passed the offices of other assorted medical and mental health professionals. It was a sort of mall, the doctor had mused throughout the years. These "medical complexes" were like malls for those seeking doctors, and in essence, he was just another shoe or video game store. The idea did not bring him any sense of pride, of course, and it was likely among the factors contributing to his overall apathy about his life. He wanted—no, *needed*—to feel something, anything.

The doctor greeted his receptionist with the usual pleasant-ries and inquired as to the status of his appointments for the day. Carol responded that he had four patients scheduled to see him and that his first appointment, Tessa Lubjeck, was scheduled for ten o'clock. The doctor thanked Carol and headed into his office.

Once inside, the doctor placed his briefcase on the small round coffee table in the center of the room and walked over to a closed armoire and opened the doors. Inside the armoire on a center shelf was a large antique metronome. The doctor picked up the metronome, wound it, and placed it back on the shelf before removing the wooden front cover to reveal the pendulum. From a small wooden box on a shelf above the metronome, the doctor removed two medium-sized votive candles, and after placing the wooden box back onto its shelf, he placed one of the candles on either side of the metronome. Once these tasks were complete, the doctor shifted his attention to the other side of the room. In a position slightly catty-corner, there was a brown leather couch of the classic design. The doctor adjusted the angle of the piece of furniture until it was more or less facing the armoire squarely. The last item that warranted the doctor's attention was the ther-mostat. The doctor had worked with Tessa on many occasions and knew that she tended to be more responsive with the office on the warm side, so the doctor adjusted the thermostat up from sixty-eight degrees to seventy-five degrees.

With these preparations made, the doctor picked up his briefcase and took a seat at his desk. Once seated, he opened his briefcase, removed a yellow legal pad, closed the briefcase, and placed it on the floor to the left of his chair. The legal pad was new, only the top page having been used. On this page, in the doctor's blocky handwriting, was the script he would use in the upcoming session with Tessa. He would often do a hypnotherapy session without such a script, as he had been doing this for decades, but in cases where he was trying a new strategy for a session, he would sometimes work from a carefully written script. In this case, he definitely wanted to be on point with the criteria he had gleaned from the Greyson Scale and the Weighted Core Experience Index.

After reading the script over, satisfied with it, the doctor checked his watch. It was 9:25 a.m. Thirty-five minutes till Tessa was scheduled to arrive. The doctor had a bad case of butterflies. A series of worrisome thoughts entered his mind. What if Tessa cancelled the appointment at the last minute? What if she opted to forgo hypnosis this session and just wanted to talk? Tessa had never cancelled an appointment, so that was unlikely, but there had been occasions in which she had preferred to simply talk things through. The doctor decided he would have to take things as they came, and if necessary, guide Tessa toward a hypnotherapy session.

The doctor, very conscious of his state of anxiety, closed his eyes and began to breathe deeply. As he did this, he began to repeat a mantra to himself quietly, "Let go. Be calm." As the doctor did this, he could feel his nervous energy start to dissipate. It was a coping mechanism he had used over the years during times of stress and uncertainty, and his emotional muscle memory had grown very susceptible to its effects.

The sound of Carol's voice over the intercom broke his meditative state. "Doctor, your ten o'clock appointment is here."

The doctor, somewhat startled, shook his head and checked his watch. The time was 9:47!

"Thanks, Carol. Send her in, please." The doctor leaned forward and hit the blinking Line 2 button.

He rose from his chair, walked to his office door, and opened it to Tessa's smiling face.

"Hi, Doctor!" Tessa said, warmly greeting him.

"Tessa! So good to see you. Come on in." He extended his hand to Tessa. She took it, clasping it between both of hers and shaking it slowly. After Tessa released his hand, the doctor motioned to the chairs placed near the coffee table.

"Have a seat, please," he said as he closed the office door. Tessa sat down, and the doctor took a seat in the chair next to her. This was old hat in his profession, something referred to as "sympathetic position," intended to be less confrontational than sitting directly in front of the patient or, heaven forbid, addressing him or her from across his desk. The doctor had unconsciously even mimicked Tessa's posture and position in her chair, another method used to read the emotional state of a patient.

It was clear that if the doctor had experienced a bit of nerves earlier, they had passed, and he was on a sort of autopilot, doing what he had done thousands of times during his career. "So. How've you been lately, Tessa?" he asked.

Tessa took a breath, let it out, and with an upward glance, replied, "Well, Doctor, I just got back from the cruise I told you about during our last session."

"Sure. I remember. How was it?"

Tessa shifted around in her chair, crossing her right leg over her left as she turned slightly toward the doctor before answering.

"It was good. Overall, it was good, but..." Tessa paused, searching for words.

"But?" the doctor said, chuckling softly. "Go ahead, Tessa. You know the drill. Open and honest."

Tessa smiled sheepishly, nodded, and went on.

"Open and honest. Sure. But I found that some of my anxiety showed itself. Not over-the-top like before, mind you, but noticeable."

The doctor nodded slowly, knowingly, and then smiled.

"It was your first time in a really social situation in a while," the doctor said soothingly. "The fact that you describe the experience as 'good overall' is real progress, don't you think?"

Tessa smiled and nodded. "No. You're right, Doctor. Sure."

The doctor returned Tessa's smile. "Remember, we can't judge progress from where we are but only compare it with how far we've come. With that context in mind, would you say that the cruise was a positive experience?"

Tessa looked slightly upward again as if measuring the question. Once her eyes came back down, a smile came across her face. "Looking at it that way, I'd say yes. It was a positive experience. Looking back on it, I had a lot of fun."

"Great! Just great, Tessa. I'm glad for you." The doctor reached over and patted Tessa's hand gently. "How would you feel about a little booster, Tessa? A tune-up, if you will? It sounds like you're doing great, and it's my opinion that if what we're doing is useful for you, we should keep moving forward. What do you think?"

Tessa nodded immediately, a smile on her face. "Absolutely!" she replied brightly. "You're the doctor."

"Okay. You know the drill, Tessa. Go ahead and recline on the couch over there. Make yourself comfortable."

Tessa walked over and reclined on the couch. The doctor moved his chair to a position parallel and slightly to the rear of the couch, a position again used out of habit. He then walked to the armoire and, using a lighter he produced from his pocket, lit both of the candles. The doctor then walked across the room and, using the light switch near the door, turned out the lights. Besides a bit of light coming in around the curtains covering the windows on either side of the armoire, the room was lit only by the warm light of the flickering votive candles flanking the metronome.

"Are you comfortable, Tessa?" the doctor asked, standing at the doorway.

"Yes, very comfortable, thanks," Tessa replied.

"Warm enough? I know you like it on the warm side."

"Oh. Yes. Very comfortable."

"Wonderful," the doctor answered.

The doctor then walked to his desk, opened the top drawer, and retrieved a small, clip-on LED reading light and the yellow legal pad with his session script. He then took a seat in the chair to the left of the couch Tessa was reclining on, attached the LED light to the legal pad, and adjusted the light so it would provide just enough illumination for him to read without distracting Tessa. He placed the legal pad on the floor to the left of his chair and stepped to the armoire. "Okay, Tessa, are you all set? Comfortable?"

"All set, Doctor," Tessa replied.

He turned his attention to the metronome; he released the pendulum and slid it down four clicks. "This is where you usually like it, but let me know if it's too slow, too fast." The doctor stepped to the side as the pendulum on the metronome began swaying from one side to the other, clicking its mechanical rhythm.

"How's that, Tessa?" the doctor asked softly.

Tessa nodded slowly in the affirmative, having already locked her gaze on the swaying pendulum. Tessa, like the doctor's other long-term patients, had become quite susceptible to the process. The doctor nodded, walked over to his chair, quietly seated himself, and picked up the legal pad.

"Okay, Tessa. From here on out, you will keep your eyes locked onto that gently swaying pendulum. Listen to the calming rhythm of the metronome. Nothing else exists. Just that golden, swaying pendulum." His voice was low and even, calm. "Concentrate, Tessa. All of your attention, all of your focus, on that gently swaying pendulum. As you concentrate more and more deeply, you feel yourself becoming more and more relaxed, your breathing becoming easier, calmer."

The doctor could see Tessa's eyes growing heavier as he watched her through his peripheral vision. And he went on.

"As you concentrate, focus all of your attention on that sway-ing pendulum. As you listen to the gentle sound of the metro-nome, you feel your eyes becoming very heavy. The deeper you concentrate, focus your attention on the pendulum, the more relaxed you feel. Your eyes are growing impossibly heavy, Tessa, as if they are being pulled down. Your arms, legs, and body so calm, so relaxed, they feel like lead."

Tessa's posture in the chair was becoming looser, her head slowly dipping, her eyes barely open. Suddenly, Tessa's eyes closed, and her body fell loose on the couch.

"Good. Good, Tessa. You're feeling calm and safe and warm and relaxed, but we're going to go deeper. We're going to go fur-ther, more relaxed than you've ever felt. No matter how deep we go, Tessa, you will always be able to hear and respond to the sound of my voice."

The doctor always used that last sentence to ensure the patient would be able to come out of the hypnotic state when cued to at the end of the session. It was possible there would be no coming out of this session, and the addition of the words by the doctor was another example of habits formed over decades of doing this work.

"In a moment, I'm going to begin a countdown, and as I say the number, you're going to see it flash in front of you in your mind's eye. Ten. The numbers grow smaller and smaller as the countdown continues. Nine. You're going to feel yourself slipping deeper and deeper into a state of total, relaxed calm. Eight. As the numbers grow smaller, you're slipping more and more deeply into a state of calm emptiness. Seven. Everything letting go, your body flowing into the floor like water. Six. Deeper, farther, more

SIX TALES FROM PURGATORY

relaxed than ever before. Five. As the countdown continues, you feel all thought and feeling leaving you, replaced by a feeling of calm emptiness. Four. Further, deeper. Three. Calmer than ever before, impossibly relaxed, safe. Two. A state of total and complete safety, calm. One."

The word "one" was said in voice that was a bit sharper and higher than the rest of the countdown, the subtle emphasis added to anchor the patient to this state of being. Tessa's body was completely loose; her head lolled to one side, the rise and fall of her chest slow and steady. The doctor turned his attention to the legal pad and his script.

"So calm. So safe. You're drifting in the warm, quiet darkness, Tessa. In this darkness, in the calm, there is no time. Your mind is flooded with thoughts, ideas. In your mind, Tessa, surrounding you in this warm, safe darkness, you can see and feel all of the events of your life from birth to the present. People, places, events swirl through you mind and around your body. In this moment, Tessa, you feel a deep sense of understanding, of peace. All is understood. Feelings of incomparable joy wash over you, filling you up."

At this point, the doctor could see tears flowing from Tessa's eyes, down her cheeks.

"As you drift, filled with joy and understanding, you feel a powerful connection, a oneness with the universe. You are surrounded by a soft, warm, beautiful light. As you are surrounded by this light, you feel vividly as if all sensations are being experienced at once. You can see beyond sight, Tessa, beyond reality. Visions of what was, what is, what will be come to you in waves."

Behind the tears, the doctor could see Tessa's eyes darting rapidly behind their lids, a state some of his patients would enter similar to REM sleep.

"You feel that you are leaving, have left, your body, Tessa. Far below you, below the darkness, you can see your body lying on the couch. You are in a place out of this world, beyond this time. A presence is with you, around you, moving through you. An entity of timeless age and boundless power."

Tessa's breathing had become labored, her body twitching.

"There's a portal of light, and you feel yourself drawn into the portal, Tessa. You can see them welcoming you, those who have already passed. You feel so safe and welcome and warm."

Tessa's breathing grew irregular and raspy.

"You feel yourself crossing over Tessa, crossing over to the side of light. You know, you can feel, that there is no return from this place."

Tessa began to convulse mildly; then, she stopped moving. Tessa had gone limp. The doctor watched her for a moment in the dim room, looking for the rise and fall of her chest. Seeing no movement, the doctor, after glancing nervously at the door out of instinct, rose cautiously from his chair and approached Tessa. As he stood next to Tessa in the dimly lit room, he was reminded of a moment from his early childhood.

The doctor remembered going on a deer hunt with his grandfather when he was a boy and the way he and his grandfather had approached the deer his grandfather had shot.

"Is it dead, Grandpa?" the doctor remembered asking as they stood over the deer. His grandfather had not answered him until, using the barrel of his rifle, he had poked the deer a few times.

"It's dead, boy," his grandfather had replied.

The doctor reached out tentatively with his right hand and placed his index and middle finger against Tessa's throat, feeling for a pulse. Nothing. The doctor once again glanced back at the door. He leaned in close to Tessa's face, turning his right cheek and ear to face Tessa's mouth and nose. After holding this position for at least thirty seconds, the doctor determined that Tessa was not breathing and stood upright again.

He returned to his chair and took a seat, his heart beating faster. After a few moments, the doctor took a deep breath and cried out with as much anguish as he could muster, "Tessa! Tessa!"

The doctor rose from his chair, pushing it backward violently and ran to the door, flipped on the lights, opened the door, and burst into the reception area.

"Carol, call 911! Something's wrong with Tessa!" the doctor blurted out frantically. Carol sat there, staring wide-eyed at the doctor.

"Carol! Goddamn it! Call 911! I think Tessa's had a heart attack or something!" the doctor repeated, slapping both palms on the startled woman's desktop. Carol, her stupor broken, picked up her phone's receiver and dialed. As Carol spoke with the 911 operator, the doctor stumbled backward and leaned against the open doorway to his office, looking as though he might collapse.

"They're coming, Doctor!" Carol said, rising from her desk and approaching the doorway. The doctor held out his left hand, palm toward the shaken receptionist.

"No, Carol," the doctor said, his voice cracking. "Please. Please don't look. You shouldn't see this."

He stepped toward Carol and, putting his hands on her shoulders, said, "Go downstairs, Carol. Go downstairs, and meet the ambulance so they can find us."

Carol had begun to cry, so the doctor gently lifted her chin with his right hand, bringing her gaze directly into his. "Can you do this for me, Carol?" the doctor asked her tenderly. She nodded weakly, tears streaming down her face.

"Good. That's good. Go on, now. Go." The doctor moved Carol toward the exit. Once Carol was on her way, the doctor took a seat in one of the reception area chairs, loosened his tie, mussed his hair, and placed his hands on his knees. The paramedics would find him like this, sitting disheveled, staring blankly ahead, looking dazed. It would be a simple narrative. They were in session when Tessa began showing signs of distress. It was so quick, he would say, he had tried to rouse her but was unable to, so he rushed out and asked his faithful receptionist, Carol, to call for help.

There was no reason they would question his account, no outward sign of foul play. It would be confirmed that Tessa had experienced a cardiac event and had died as a result of it. Only the doctor would know that he had killed her, that he had entered her mind and talked, coaxed Tessa's life, her soul, from her body.

Bound

"And so, as we think about the funerary ritual known as 'Sky Burial,' we must let go of our Western, postmodern, limited view of death," the professor said, holding his hands open at either side of his head. He was distracted, but he continued. "The very modern, industrial idea that death is somehow bad or unclean keeps us from appreciating the beauty, the truth of these sorts of rituals," he said, brushing an errant strand of hair from his eye. The professor was thirty-five, leanly built, and handsome. He wore his sandy-blond hair in a samurai-style bun and sported leather, open-toed sandals, faded jeans, and an untucked plaid shirt to complete his look, the look of the accessible, progressive, young professor.

He had grown used to attention from his female students, who almost universally found him attractive in a physical, intellectual, and social sense. It was curious that the source of his distraction was a young woman in his classroom. The young woman in question was not a student of his, had no business in his class, and had made it clear on previous occasions that she was not a great fan of his. It was also of note that Tasha, the young woman in question, was the best friend of his most recent ex-girlfriend, Elizabeth.

As the professor continued his lecture on the limitations of the Western mind to understand traditional indigenous funerary practices, he was repeatedly drawn to Tasha, sitting in the front row. First of all, Tasha was very attractive. Tall, with long, beautiful legs, which she displayed prominently from beneath a very short skirt, Tasha was looking at him with her big brown eyes. Her eyes were made even more noticeable by Tasha's hair, dark brown and short cropped, giving her a decidedly pixieish look.

Second of all, Tasha seemed to be putting off some fairly flirty signals. The professor had dated Tasha's friend Elizabeth for six months, and during that time, his only interactions with Tasha had been cold, glaring stares when he'd visited their apartment. These interactions had always been fleeting, as Tasha always chose to leave the apartment when he visited. He remembered asking Elizabeth about "the Tasha situation," as he called it one night. His theory was that Tasha was infatuated with Elizabeth in a romantic way and was jealous of their relationship, and he had asked Elizabeth about it. Elizabeth had responded with laughter at the idea.

"Oh my God, William! No! That's definitely not what's going on with her," Elizabeth had explained. "She's definitely not a lesbian. Jeez, I can't believe you actually went there. That's the explanation you came up with? Do you not think it possible that there is a woman who *doesn't* find you charming?" she had said, giggling.

"No. I mean, I don't think every woman finds me charming." he'd responded, his ego feeling a bit bruised. "What is it, then? I mean, I haven't spoken ten words to the girl, and she looks at me like she wants to punch me in the throat."

Elizabeth had put her hands on his shoulders and playfully smiled at him. "If I tell you, you have to promise not to bring it up to her. She is my best friend, after all. I can't have my boyfriend and my best friend at each other's throats, okay?"

"Sure. I promise. I won't bring it up. Not that she would talk to me, anyway."

"You promise, William?"

"I promise. Lay it on me. And for the record, I'm not that egotistical," he'd said, giving Elizabeth his best puppy eyes.

"Okay. Here goes. Tasha thinks you're a player. She doesn't think I should trust you. She says you don't have the best reputation as far as dating your students."

William remembered feeling his stomach drop at those words and consciously trying not to look busted. Despite the risks, he had dated a lot of his students but had always been able to keep things discreet enough to avoid any repercussions; students came and went, and he was adept at manipulating the young and naive. William feigned a surprised expression before responding.

"Wow! I mean, just, wow! I thought this was the twenty-first century. So I should be a stereotypical person and just marry and fit into the social norm? I mean, damn! I'm not allowed to explore relationships because of my job title?" William had turned up a tone of indignation in his voice, looking down, shaking his head as if in disbelief of what he was hearing.

"William! Don't be like that. She doesn't know you like I do," Elizabeth had said, putting her hands on his cheeks and looking into his eyes with a tender expression.

"No, you're right, hon. It just stings to be painted like that. No other professor on this campus has pushed for women's rights, for equality, like I have, all the marches, petitions, and protests. I mean, really. Talk about being judged." As he spoke, he had slowly shaken his head as if in a state of total disbelief.

"I know all of that, William," Elizabeth had said. "You are the most wonderful man I have ever met. Certainly the best boyfriend I've ever had. Please don't hold it against her. She's just really protective of her friends. She'll come around."

With this memory in his mind, William finished his lecture, all the while very conscious of the sultry looks he was getting from Tasha. As students emptied from the lecture hall, Tasha remained in her seat, and as William gathered his papers at the podium, he could feel her looking at him. With his papers in his courier bag, William walked toward the front row. He really wanted to know what Tasha was doing here, what she wanted, so he walked up to her seat. Tasha looked totally relaxed, mischievous even. Before he could say a word, Tasha spoke.

"Hello, William," she said, a sly smile on her face.

"Hello, Tasha. I didn't know you had an interest in funerary practices. What brings you here?" William asked, bracing himself.

"I don't have an interest in funerary practices. But I do have an interest in you, to answer your question," she replied seductively.

William thought the response vague, and, afraid she was going to go into a tirade about him breaking her best friend's heart, he decided to head her off. "Look, Tasha, I know you don't like me. Elizabeth made that clear. So if you're here on her behalf or just to get your digs in, I don't want to hear it. Elizabeth is a grown woman, and besides that, this is between the two of us, and frankly, it isn't any of your business."

Tasha laughed and shook her head, her big, dark eyes twinkling.

"What's so funny, Tasha?" William was getting irritated.

"Elizabeth told you I didn't like you, huh?" Tasha said, smiling.

"Yes, she did. So no need to elaborate on that."

"Of course I told her I didn't like you, William," Tasha said. "I certainly wasn't going to tell my best friend I thought her boyfriend was hot."

William looked confused. "What?" he asked.

"You really think the reason I never spoke to you, never hung around when you came to visit her, was because I didn't like you? Believe me, if I didn't like you, I would have just told you. I love Beth, but I really don't know what you saw in her. I know it's wrong, but what do they say? The heart wants what the heart wants."

William was going from a state of confusion to arousal. "Are you serious? What about Elizabeth?" William asked, his voice lower, almost teasing.

Tasha suddenly stood up, pulled William in, and kissed him. Feeling her body against his, her tongue in his mouth, William was definitely aroused. Tasha pulled away, and as she walked past him, she turned to William. "To answer your question, you broke up with Beth, so no problem there, and if you want to know how serious I am, come to the apartment tonight at seven. Beth will be indisposed, so don't worry about that. I'll pick up a bottle of wine. You in?"

William had a sly smile on his face, still feeling the effect of the unexpected kiss. "I'll be there, Tasha. Looking forward to it."

"Not as much as I am, William. You have no idea." Tasha gave him a wink.

William watched Tasha as she walked away, imagining what was under that short skirt at the end of those long legs.

William arrived a few minutes early. The date was relatively brief. William had gotten through his second glass of wine and was feeling unusually tipsy as Tasha took him by the hand and led him to the bedroom. William was somewhat surprised to find himself led to Elizabeth's room, but who was he to refuse? Once in the dark room, he vaguely remembered Tasha moving behind him as he stepped in.

"Let me get the lights," Tasha said.

As the light came on, William remembered two things. The first was the sight of Elizabeth's body sitting upright against the bed. She looked so pale. Her eyes were open, and it was clear from the amount of blood and the wounds on her forearms that she had died as a result of cutting both wrists. The second thing William remembered was that before he could react, he'd felt a searing pain and had lost all control of his body.

"Wake up, asshole!" William could faintly hear a voice saying, as though the person were far away. "Seriously. Wake the fuck up, douchebag!"

William felt a sharp blow to his back, and his eyes fluttered as he started to come to.

"For the love of Christ!"

William could hear clearly now that it was Tasha.

"Wake up!" he heard again.

A moment later, William felt himself doused with cold water.

"Aaagh! Uhhhh! Okay! Okay!" William stammered.

Upon opening his eyes, William was greeted by Elizabeth—or, more precisely, Elizabeth's face—inches from his own. Strangely enough, it took a moment for him to register what he was seeing. Elizabeth's dead eyes stared from her pale face, her mouth slightly agape.

"Aaaagh! Nooo! No! Oh, my God! Nooo!" William screamed, trying to move away from the dead girl. William found himself unable to move and had closed his eyes, not wanting to look at her.

"Save it, Billy boy!" William heard Tasha say, giving him another kick to the back.

"Okay! Okaaay!" William sobbed. "Please stop, Tasha! You don't have to do this! What are you doing? It's too much! Please!"

Tasha had stepped around so she could see William's face. Tasha knelt down and was patting William on the head. William kept his eyes closed.

"You're right. It is too much," Tasha said calmly. "That fucking man-bun you wear, definitely too much. What a complete tool you are. Do you know that? I warned Beth again and again about you. Love goggles, I swear."

William had started to cry, his eyes still tightly shut, a low whimper like a child's emanating from his mouth.

"Open your eyes, Billy," Tasha commanded calmly.

"No. For God's sake, no. I can't!" William sobbed.

Tasha grabbed William's hair by the man-bun and shook his head violently.

"If you don't open your eyes, I swear I'll cut your fucking eyelids off, you piece of shit!" Tasha screamed.

"No! Please don't! I'll open my eyes! Please!" William pleaded, his eyes blinking open as if to mitigate the view of Elizabeth's dead face. By tilting his face to the right, William could see past Elizabeth enough to see Tasha kneeling on the other side of her, a knife in her right hand.

"Don't you look at me, you sack of shit! Look at her! Look at her, or those eyelids are coming off," Tasha said, once again shaking his head.

"Okay! Okay! I'll look at her! Don't cut me, please!" William cried. William was looking directly into Elizabeth's eyes. There was nothing there but the emptiness of death. Elizabeth's eyes had begun to cloud slightly. William had resumed his whimpering.

"She was my best friend, William. I loved her. I know you didn't, that you never did. She was so good. Too good for a shit-head like you."

William's whimpering had increased, and he had once again closed his eyes.

"You motherfucker!" Tasha bellowed, reaching down and cutting off part of William's right ear. William issued a high-pitched scream.

"Open your fucking eyes right fucking now, Billy," Tasha said coldly. "If I have to tell you again, off go the eyelids. Try me if you don't believe me."

"Okay! Okay! Okay! Okay!" William said emphatically, opening his eyes and staring into Elizabeth's.

"Are we tracking, Billy? You going to keep those eyes open and that whiny mouth of yours shut and let me talk?" Tasha said, letting go of William's man-bun and crouching down lower to look at him.

"Yes. I understand. Okay. Okay," William stammered.

"Good. I don't want to be here all night, for fuck's sake. I had to find her like that, William. My best friend. My sister."

If William could have seen Tasha's face clearly, he would have seen tears streaming down her cheeks as she spoke.

"She loved you, William. She thought you were the one. She was always going on about how much you fought for women, how you were so different from other men. But you know what I think, William?" Tasha asked.

William was silent, breathing coarsely. Tasha began poking the tip of her knife into his forehead, a tap, tap, tap like a woodpecker boring into a tree, which immediately brought blood and another scream from William.

"Don't be so fucking rude, Billy! We're having a conversation, here. I require an answer when I ask you a question. So, again, you want to know what I think of you?"

"Yes. Tell me," William sputtered.

"Great. I think you are a total fake, a liar, a poser. You can go to all of the woman's marches you want, protest all you want, wear a fucking pussy hat if you want to. It's all a con. It's all just another way for you to get laid. You have no respect whatever for women. You just have a nice, politically correct pickup line. I'm so progressive. I'm for women's equality, blah, blah, blah. So when Beth came to you two days ago and told you she was pregnant, you thought the most respectful course of action was to break up with her? You told her it wasn't your problem. You killed my best friend, you piece of garbage! You crushed her like you've crushed so many of your students. It's your fucking problem now, though, isn't it, asshole?"

William needed no prompting from the knife this time and answered Tasha straightaway. "Yeah. Yes, it is. It is. I'm so sorry. So sorry," William sobbed.

Tasha grabbed William by the bun once more and leaned in close.

"What did you say, Billy? Sorry for what? Sorry to whom?" Tasha snapped.

"I'm so sorry, Elizabeth, so sorry. Sorry for treating you like that. I never thought anything like this would happen. I'm so sorry," William said between sobs.

Tasha pulled away and, tilting her head to one side, said, "See, William? That wasn't so hard, was it?"

William stopped sobbing for a moment. "Will you please forgive me, Tasha? Please let me go. I promise, I won't say anything. Please, I swear. I'm so sorry for Elizabeth." William had lapsed back into sobs as he pled.

Tasha began laughing hysterically. "Holy shit, do you have some nerve! Are you off of your meds? You're here to stay, Billy! But on the bright side, you should find this beautiful, or ironic, or beautifully ironic. Elizabeth told me about some tribe you talked about from the Pacific Northwest. She said that sometimes when a chief died, a living slave would be bound to the chief's body and left there to expire. She said you told her it could take days for the slave to die. I'm sure with your enlightened mind, you'll be able to see the beauty, the poetry of this."

"No! Please, Tasha, don't do this! Someone will find out! It's not too late! Please! Please!" William begged.

"Here we go, William. Let me explain a few things to you. First, I know you didn't tell a goddamned soul you were coming to the apartment. Beth used to go on about how no one could know about your relationship with her because you were her professor. Second, you are in an undisclosed location in the middle of West Virginia on private land. It's the middle of summer, and there won't be any hunters here till September."

"Nooo! Tasha don't!" William interrupted.

Tasha stepped around to William's back and delivered a savage kick to his ribs.

"Do not interrupt me, asshole," Tasha said calmly.

William was gasping to catch his breath as Tasha continued.

"Okay. Let's see. Also, I used like five rolls of duct tape on you, so I am not about to go to all the trouble of cutting you out. Finally, and most importantly, you're an arrogant sociopath that basically killed my friend, so no. I'm damn well not letting you go. I will, of course, remove poor Beth after you're done for and see that she is buried with the dignity she deserves."

Tasha walked around to the feet of the bound pair. William continued to whimper and cry. Tasha closed the knife and put it in the right pocket of her jeans. As she scanned the forest to the south, the sun was getting higher. Tasha checked her watch.

"Ten fifteen. Wow, time for me to go. I've got quite a hike ahead of me, and according to the forecast, it's going to get pretty warm today. Goodbye, William," Tasha said, turning to walk away.

"Fucking bitch!" William shrieked. "You're just another stupid cunt! You won't get away with this! You'll see, you bitch!"

Tasha stopped and turned her head to look back at William.

"There it is. The real William. Enjoy your time here," Tasha said calmly over her shoulder. She resumed walking, and as she continued on, the sound of William's cursing and screaming grew fainter and fainter until she could hear nothing but the sound of birds and her own footfalls in the leaf litter.

For William, the days ahead passed slowly. As the sun rose higher, it got hotter, more humid. William struggled hard for the first couple of hours, but soon gave up in exhaustion. The thick layers of duct tape seemed to be getting tighter as the day wore on, and in another moment of horror, William realized it was because Elizabeth's body was starting to bloat slowly in the oppressive heat. Flies, big blue bottles, had begun to arrive by the time the sun had started its afternoon descent, and by evening, their incessant buzzing and crawling added yet another element to William's discomfort.

William passed out sometime after the sun had set, but he was awakened by a tugging feeling. William opened his eyes, trying to discern the cause of the movement in the inky darkness. At this point, he was beyond feeling anything in his extremities due to the tightness of his bindings and could only move his head slightly, trying to avoid contact with Elizabeth's face. William listened, still feeling the sensation of being tugged at. He could hear leaves rustling behind Elizabeth's back. An animal. It was an animal of some kind pulling at Elizabeth's body.

"Aaagh! Go away! Goddamn it! Get!" William screamed, resuming his struggle weakly.

Startled by William's outburst, whatever it was, ran off into the night. William listened to the sound of the animal moving away and hoped it wouldn't return. On and off for the rest of the night, William struggled between passing out from exhaustion and staying awake to ward off more animals. There were times that William could hear things moving in the darkness. Most disconcerting to him were the times when the sounds came from behind him.

Sometime the next morning, William was roused by the sun shining through the canopy of leaves overhead. He had a headache, most likely from dehydration, and his mouth was dry. He wanted to resume his struggle against the layers of tape but had no strength. William was so cold, part of him was hoping for the sun to hurry its journey into the sky to provide him with some warmth. Elizabeth's eyes had completely clouded over, and the skin of her face had turned blotchy, with big, strawberry-colored patches. The flies were back in force, their horde buzzing and crawling, buzzing and crawling. William blinked his eyes and blew feebly from his mouth and nose to keep them out, but he could do nothing about his ears. As for Elizabeth, the flies were entering and exiting freely from her mouth and nostrils. As exhausted as William was, the flies' persistent efforts made even passing out difficult.

After the sun had made its way higher—perhaps it was noon—William was startled by something big, some kind of bird landing in the treetops above. It was soon joined by others, and eventually one landed within his limited field of vision. Vultures. Big, black-headed vultures were gathering in the trees above them. The smell of death, somehow not perceived by William, had made its way up into the thermals, had been picked up by the vultures and guided them there. William was becoming frantic, and his anxiety heightened when one of the great, black birds glided to the ground and began to make its way toward them.

"Go away! Aaaarr!" William yelled, his parched throat feeling as though it would crack under the effort. A cloud of blue bottles rose with a start. With some unused reserve of strength, William tried to wriggle his body. The startled bird retreated upward and took a perch among its brethren in the canopy. William was suddenly assailed by a nauseating smell as a hiss escaped Elizabeth's mouth, gas from her decomposing organs blowing directly into William's face. William retched and gagged, and finally, unable to control himself, he vomited. William could hear the vultures taking flight as he spit and tried to clear his throat, and as he did this, he was continually making contact with Elizabeth's face, adding to his revulsion.

For the remainder of the second day, William struggled against the flies, his thirst, the increasingly brazen vultures, and Elizabeth's stare. As the sun began to set, the vultures retreated to their perches, and the flies dissipated. William was so thirsty, so tired, his nose so assailed by the smell of rot and his own vomit, that at long last, he again passed out. While unconscious, William began to dream. In his dream, he was back at the lecture hall talking to his students about sky burial.

"And so, after the body has been dismembered and the proper rituals performed, the corpse is laid out on the rocks to be taken up by the vultures," William explained to his students. As he tried to continue the lecture, someone was tugging at his right shoulder.

"One moment. I'll be with you in a moment. Let me finish this. Hey, that hurts!" William said to the unseen person tugging at his shoulder. As he turned to see who was accosting him as he gave his lecture, he saw nothing, but the painful tugging at his right shoulder continued. William opened his eyes, wide awake from the dream. Something was pulling at this right shoulder. Something was biting him, tearing at him!

"Aaagh! Get off me!" William screamed with as much volume as his exhaustion would allow. Whatever it was beat a hasty retreat. For the remainder of the night, William's terror at the thought of being eaten alive as well as the searing pain in his shoulder would not allow him to sleep. It became clear later that night that it had been a pack of coyotes. William could hear them yipping and sparring excitedly in the woods around them for several hours. If William heard footfalls coming in, he would yell weakly, and they would retreat. William knew he was fading, growing weaker. Thirst would kill him unless the animals got around to it first. This much he knew. Three days without water was about it for a human. In the back of his mind, William entertained the idea that Tasha would return, and after giving him a final dressing-down, release him. The rational part of him knew this was unlikely. The fact that she had bound him to her friend's corpse was a sure sign that this woman meant business.

As the darkness began to retreat, the coyotes vanished, and William fell into a black, dreamless unconsciousness. William's respite was short-lived, however, as not long after the sun broke over the horizon, the flies returned, buzzing and crawling. They seemed to have an affinity for Elizabeth's eyes, he mused, and at times the entire surface of them would be covered by a mass of insects, giving her an inhuman appearance. Dark, vile liquid had begun to ooze from her mouth and nose, and her lips had begun to retreat away from her teeth.

The vultures returned before noon, or perhaps they had been there all night, but he didn't hear them. He wasn't sure if he could even yell at this point, so he decided to try before the vultures began their forays.

"Goak...go. Gah," was about all he could manage, and only at a medium volume. William knew he couldn't struggle physically anymore. He couldn't even feel his arms and legs. He couldn't even shoo the flies from his nose, mouth, and eyes anymore. The bindings were probably looser since Elizabeth's eruption, but he couldn't tell one way or another. He heard several of the vultures come to ground, and this time, they would not be denied. William could only watch in complete horror as they came closer, looking almost comical with their awkward vulture walk. One of them began to pick at Elizabeth's back.

William wanted to cry, but he didn't even have that in him. The beginning of day three, the end was near. Suddenly William felt his right ear, the one Tasha had cut, being pulled at. Part of it gave way, and the vulture took it. In spite of the searing pain, William could manage little in response.

"Eeeeeeaaah." A little stifled version of a scream escaped his lips. As more of the vultures joined in, the flies protested by swarming to and fro, buzzing and buzzing, landing, crawling, and flying. William could feel the vultures tearing at his back and legs in the areas not covered by the duct tape. It was over. The vultures might not kill him, but the coyotes, and other things, as well, would be around tonight, and there was nothing he could do to stop them. As William contemplated his agony, he looked into Elizabeth's fly-eyes, at her blotchy face. She was smiling at him, a big, toothy smile, her lips drawn tight over her dead face.

"You got me, girl," William thought. "I got you, and you got me."

Author Biography

Paul S. Fowler is an author and former mental health professional from Randolph County, West Virginia. His family settled in the Potomac Highlands area in the mid-1700s and Fowler has always cultivated a great love and respect for the land. He is an avid reader (especially of horror), a keen fly fisherman, and a master falconer. Those passions drive several of the short stories in his new collection, Six Tales From Purgatory. Fowler has three adult children. He lives with his wife and youngest son in a century-old farmhouse in the countryside of Monroe County, West Virginia. Fowler also enjoys reading history and frequenting drive-in theaters.

The End

www.ingramcontent.com/pod-product-compliance
Lightning Source LLC
Chambersburg PA
CBHW021041130626
46552CB00005B/1958